Also by M.E. Kemp:

Who poisoned the Patroon's nephew with a deadly dose of brandy? Someone defiled the drink of LAURENS DE NOYES so that the drunken Dutchman dropped dead on Boston Common. Widowed businesswoman Hetty Henry teams up with young Boston minister Increase "Creasy" Cotton to investigate Colonial Albany for suspects.

Could it be the wife, ANNEKE VAN KLEECK, who keeps her own name and her cool at news of her husband's death? Could it be Anneke's father, OLD MYNDERT VAN KLEECK, who detested his philandering son-in-law?

Lovely DIANA CAMPBELL was jilted by de Noyes for the older, wealthier Anneke and Diana's Dad, DR. CAMPBELL's mistress was stolen by the devious Dutchman. De Noyes threatened to expose a massive land fraud by the County Clerk, LUCIUS MONTGOMERY and Montgomery's secretary, the young Scot ALEXANDER MACLEOD, puts Hetty in a chilly predicament. De Noyes' two guides to Boston, genial GERRITT VAN WIESAL and Harvard-educated Mohawk BILLY BLUE BEAR, had every opportunity to lace the liquor. Even the Patroon, KILLIAN VAN RENSSELAER, fought with de Noyes over who owned a fertile farm. In fact, the only one with no motive to do in de Noyes is the shady Manhattanite ALPHONSE DELAHOUSIE, the person most agreeable to dispatching an opponent—any opponent. Hetty and Creasy undergo Indian attack, kidnapping and Piracy on the High Hudson before they uncork the criminal with a doctored dram of their own.

Death of a Bawdy Belle

*For Carol —
a tiny dancer
From M. E. Kemp
a merry murderer!*

M.E. Kemp

HILLIARD HARRIS

HILLIARD HARRIS

P.O. Box 275
Boonsboro, Maryland 21713-0275

First Edition-April 2008
ISBN 1-59133-235-4
978-1-59133-235-0

Book Design: S. A. Reilly
Cover Illustration © S. A. Reilly
Manufactured/Printed in the United States of America
2008

For Cappy and Buddy—Semper Fi

CHARACTERS

Creasy (Increase) Cotton—minister of a poor Boston church, cousin of Cotton Mather.

Hetty Henry—a nosy Puritan widow and businesswoman with many connections.

Phillip Boynton—Boston bookseller in private business.

Arabella Edwards—Hung in Salem but not a witch.

Celia Edwards—Young daughter of the hanging victim, **Arabella Edwards**.

Ferret (Eliphalet)—Young boy recruited to spy for Hetty.

Gabriel Germaine—Wealthy Huguenot refugee.

Oliver Hacker—Business agent, acts for the Edwards' estate.

Harry Kegleigh—Boston merchant.

Geoffrey Malbone—A doctor and a friend of Kegleigh.

Ephrata Phinny—Esther's son, a merchant.

Sarah Stiles—A dangerous tattletale.

Esther Thripenny—Elderly housekeeper for Arabella Edwards.

"Which witch is which?" The question hung in the early morning mist as the sheriff's assistant leaned upon his spade, his mild blue eyes focused upon the gallows above.

Sheriff George Corwin scratched his head. Two hooded figures hung like cocoons from the wooden bar; arms tied against bodies, petticoats neatly bound against the nether limbs for modesty's sake. Sheriff Corwin had only hung one witch yesterday, and that witch properly tried by the court. How did the other one come to be up there? Who dared usurp his authority to hang a duly convicted culprit?

True enough, the jails were overcrowded with witches, but if someone durst think to relieve the congestion by sneaking them out behind his back—well, that someone would soon discover that the law in the person of George Corwin, Sheriff of Salem, was not to be thwarted. He cleared his throat and spat upon the ground.

"Cut 'em down," Corwin ordered, his brows knit into a fierce scowl. "We'll see which witch is which."

The assistant shrugged, climbed up the gallows ladder and slashed at the ropes with a long knife. Two bodies dropped with flat thuds into the cart beneath. The assistant leaped down from the ladder and busied himself cutting away the ropes from each hood. When he pulled off the first one, a waxen face grinned up at him, the head lolling to one side. The strong hemp noose had snapped the neck, like shucking peas from a pod. Silvering brown hair hung in lank, loose strands around the grinning face of the corpse. Months in jail had blunted the charms of Mistress Bishop, she whose spirit-shape haunted the bridal beds of so many good and true men of Salem village.

"That's the witch I hung," Corwin muttered.

The assistant pulled off the second hood. A cascade of golden hair spilled out. Wisps covered the face that might have been a child in size and shape but looked more akin to a battered doll. The bright blue eyes bulged red-streaked, and tiny scratches crisscrossed the waxen skin. A blue-tinged tongue hung from full, bloodless lips.

"Amateur." Sheriff Corwin snorted at the hangman's incompetence. "This one danced a jig."

"Know her?" The assistant raised thin, sandy brows.

"Not one I know."

"How she come to be here?" the assistant asked.

"I don't like it," the sheriff said. "I don't like it a-tall."

Chapter One

My mind went numb. I'd been through this before. There was my dear cousin Abigail Mather sobbing on the shoulder of her husband's lanky cousin who cooed at her with the devotion of a brown-eyed Spaniel. Meanwhile, the man who should have been cooing at Abigail lay prostrate in the dust (an expression, since Cousin Abigail is an excellent housekeeper) weeping copious tears and bewailing his fate. Cousin Cotton Mather has fallen into these bouts of melancholia ever since his father fled to England, leaving the care of the largest, wealthiest congregation in the New World in the hands of his twenty-six-year-old son.

Cotton Mather was now turned twenty-nine years and troubles have come upon him. Boston jail is filling with witches, the Salem Village jail being too small to hold all the accused. Cousin Cotton's fears of a Conspiracy from Hell to overset Christ's Kingdom Here in the Wilderness are come true. The Devil leaped in through Salem's door while Cotton Mather lay in Boston too ill and exhausted to do battle.

Abigail Mather sent for the two people she trusted the most. Unfortunately, those two people were not speaking to each other. I am Abigail's cousin, Hetty Henry. Increase Cotton is minister to a poor congregation in the South End and Cotton Mather's cousin. Last fall Creasy had taken exception to some remarks I'd made. Now I might as well be invisible for the attention he paid me. And he was paying far too much attention to Abigail. I'd had to reprimand her before for encouraging his bachelor affections; I thought she'd learned her lesson—not that Abigail Mather isn't devoted to her husband. Indeed, she dotes upon him in the most slavish way possible.

I cleared my throat twice before Creasy came to his senses and released his cousin's wife. He searched the pockets of a shabby bottle-green coat, produced a square of linen and dabbed beneath the luminous eyes of Abigail Mather.

"Now, my dear, you know what you must do," he said, still cooing at her.

"Tea?" she guessed her voice breathy and fetching.

"Yes." He beamed down at her like a benevolent sun. "And add some..."

"Comfrey leaves?" She finished the sentence at his expectant pause.

"Ye-es," Creasy crooned, chucking her under the chin.

I clutched at my stomach; a sudden spasm of nausea. Creasy had lost his fiancée over the winter. Had he reverted to his pre-fiancée mooning state over Abigail? Well, it was harmless enough but childish on his part, unless it was directed at me, to annoy me, in which case it was even more childish of him.

Abigail turned to me, placing a soft plump hand upon my arm. "Hetty, you'll explain the problem to Cousin Creasy while I run to the kitchen for the tea tray, won't you?" Abigail's eyes misted with tears. I envied her the ability to weep with such fetching results. No red nose or swollen lids for Abigail Mather.

Before I could protest that I didn't know what the problem was myself, having just returned from a business venture, Abigail scurried off down the hall. She reminded me of a plump little brown mouse.

Creasy Cotton just stood there watching Abigail as if he were a house cat.

"Creasy...." I tugged at his sleeve to force his attention.

He gave his head a little shake, as if he were awakening from a dream.

I extended my hand but he ignored my offer of truce and

turned to the staircase. He bounded up the stairs two at a time. I hurried after the man but he reached the top ahead of me and scooted into Cotton Mather's bedchamber in time to slam the door shut in my face. I heard an exclamation of fright and a swift apology from Creasy. I pushed at the door but the latch held it fast.

"Creasy," I called softly. No one acknowledged me so I put my ear to the door.

Exclamations of woe filled my hearing with murmurs of a sympathetic nature interspersed, but I could not make out any particular phrases. There was nothing for it but to wait for Abigail to come with the tea tray. He could not keep out Abigail. I heard sobbing which gradually changed in tone like a child who has forgotten why he began to cry in the first place but keeps on out of habit. The drone of Creasy's voice continued, soothing in its best ministering-comfort tactic. I rested my head against the door and closed my eyes. At the clatter of the tea cups I started.

Abigail ascended the staircase, head down, eyes upon the tea tray. I moved to the head to meet her and to hold the tray so she could announce her arrival with a soft knock and a call.

The door swung open and Abigail was whisked inside.

"Hey!" I kicked the door. I was still holding the tray.

The door opened, the tray was snatched out of my hands and the door shut before I could move.

I took a step back in the hallway from astonishment. How rude! Composing myself with ten deep breaths, I prepared to storm the fortress. The door opened once again and Increase Cotton stepped through. His brow was furrowed; his eyes were like black coal, his mouth a tight line.

I felt a twinge in my bowels. Would the man never forgive me? Did I deserve such rancor for my words, which were well intentioned?

The silence between us was painful. All he did was to stand there and glare.

"Come, sir," I said. "This is beneath you. You know my

5

habit of plain speaking. I did not mean any insult to you or to your late fiancée. I have made my apologies but I offer them again to you." How was I to know the woman would take sick and die three months after I tried to make the man see she was not the right woman for him to wed?

No response. I continued, "For the sake of our mutual cousins I ask you to set aside your anger at me. How is Cousin Cotton? I should go in and help Abigail." I gestured to the door.

Perhaps it was the name that unlocked the man's mouth but he held out a hand, palm up, in warning. "Don't go in there. Cousin Cotton needs his rest. He exhausts himself with these fits of weeping. Abigail will tend to him. I'm sorry—what were you saying?"

"I should help Abigail," I repeated.

"Before that you were speaking, but my mind was elsewhere. I'm sorry." He ran the back of his hand along his forehead.

"No matter," I said. My spirits lifted. "What troubles Cousin Cotton now? Besides the Salem business, that is. The Salem business troubles us all."

He shook his head in agreement.

"Has the number of the accused diminished since I've been away?" I asked.

"You've been away?"

"I've been to the Albany Colony. I had to attend to my affairs there and I've only just returned." I felt a certain diffidence in speaking of my trip because it was upon a voyage in my ship from that colony when we had quarreled over the unfortunate Mistress Piscopot, lately deceased.

At the mention of that frontier settlement, Creasy's face gained some animation. The hint of a smile creased his long mouth.

"How are our friends there? How are the newlyweds?"

"It's a good match. You would laugh to see Gerritt strut about like a puffed-up pigeon. He is so proud of becoming a land-holder. And Anneke looks very well. There is a softness to her face that makes her look years younger. Gerritt and Anneke are happy, I think."

Marriage had worked wonders on that strong, angular Dutchwoman. Perhaps when I reached her years I would reconsider my vow not to remarry. Two husbands lost to me were enough.

"I am glad for them." Creasy spoke simply. "You saw Blue Bear? He is well?"

"Yes. Creasy, why did Abigail summon us? Has anything happened in particular to cause this bout of nerves in Cousin Cotton? You know these vapors come upon him when he is plagued by a problem he does not feel competent to solve, although he will not admit to it."

This was not the first time Cotton Mather saddled his younger cousin with the burdens he should himself shoulder. As the Mather heir, great things were expected from Cousin Cotton, as Creasy often explained to me. Cotton's father, Increase Mather, is president of Harvard College, minister to a great congregation and a diplomat who represented the Bay Colony's interests before the throne of two kings. Perhaps the expectations for the son are unfair, as Creasy contends. All I know is that Cotton Mather will never be the man his father is, and I've known him since he married my cousin, Abigail Phillips that was. He is intelligent, I grant; he can be witty and charming—there is no doubt the ladies admire him—he writes very well, preaches an eloquent sermon, and yet he lacks the simple courage that made Increase Mather such a dangerous foe of Royal Governor Edmund Andros.

Creasy, named for his uncle Increase Mather, is too tolerant of his cousin's weak nature. As for Abigail—well, the sun rises and sets by her husband's command. Nay, not command, by his request, which would be delivered as such: "Abigail, I can't see to write this pamphlet. Would you run and set the sun in the sky, if it's no trouble to you? I don't ask for myself, my dear wife, but because what I write may be of benefit in my service to the Lord...."

I repeated: "Why did Abigail summon us?"

Creasy's mouth tightened as he considered my question, yet he did not answer.

"Why is Cousin Cotton so distraught this time?"

"They have hung a witch in Salem, the first one to be hung." Creasy paused. "They found *two* bodies hanging on the gallows. Sheriff Corwin thinks it is murder. He asks Cousin Cotton to ascertain the identity of the second woman, as it is not known in Salem or the surrounding towns. She is not one of the condemned. The sheriff believes she must come from Boston." Creasy spoke in short, hard tones.

A most unladylike whistle escaped from my mouth. So the hangings had begun, and one of them was by murder. No wonder Cousin Mather was in one of his weepy moods. No wonder Creasy looked so grim. I raised my head to examine the lean face before me. Were those tiny lines around the black-fringed eyes the beginning of wrinkles or worry?

"And you have accepted the duty of discovering the identity of the victim?" I hazarded, trying my best to keep pity from my voice.

He nodded once without speaking.

"I wonder who it can be—who is missing?" I spoke my thoughts aloud without realizing that I did so.

"I shall notify the churches, that is the first step. We shall see if any wife, mother or sister is absent from services."

I knew that Creasy did not mean to sound censorious; the man has a very gallant heart when it comes to women. His concern would be justice for the poor victim.

"That will take days," I noted, again thinking out loud.

"It can't be helped. No one has spoken to Constable Phillymort of a missing woman, Cotton tells me."

"Do we have a description? Do we have the coroner's report?" I asked

"*We* do not have any report." Creasy stressed the pronoun. *We* only know from the sheriff that the woman is—was—blond of hair and blue of eye and youthful. Perhaps sixteen years of age, the sheriff said."

"A servant girl?" I wondered. "Surely the mother and father

of a young maid would have reported their daughter missing, but they might not be so quick to notice a servant gone."

A servant could be away for any number of reasons, I mused. Visiting family, sent to care for an infirm relation, carry a message to another town, run away with an unworthy lover who had his way with the poor girl and strangled her...my imagination began to run away with me.

"How was she dressed?" I asked.

"How...how should I know? The girl is buried." Creasy glared down at me.

With charity I dismissed the glare as the good man's frustration. Once again he'd been dragooned into solving Cotton Mather's problems, and with precious little information to begin a search. I reigned in my natural impatience.

"Her clothes were not buried with her, she was interred in a shroud, I'm sure," I reminded the minister.

Clothing was too expensive to waste. It was passed down through generations. Even rags could be washed and utilized again and again. I must see the girl's clothing. The garments would tell me her station in life, among other facets of her personality.

"I must have those clothes," I said.

"Now Hetty..." Creasy raised his hands as if to defend himself from my fists.

What nonsense. I've never struck the man in my life...just given him a kick or two when he needed it.

"Send for the clothing," I repeated.

"I shall make a request to the sheriff in Salem."

Creasy's mouth broke its grim line, the corners of his lips drooping like a basset hound. His hands dropped to his sides in defeat.

Smart man...perhaps he's finally admitted that I get what I'm after, although I am a mere female.

Chapter Two

I accepted the parcel with eager hands, curiosity a fault in my character with which I have had to atone for all of my life. It was good of Creasy to deliver it himself. I gave him a mug of cider and a dozen ginger cookies, which I knew were his favorite treat. He'd also brought a copy of the coroner's report. I read it with great interest while Creasy filled his lanky frame with cookies.

"Twenty-five years and she'd borne children. How could the sheriff think she was sixteen?" My question was meant to be rhetorical.

"She must have looked very young for her age," Creasy said.

I glared at the man, having recently passed my twenty-fifth birthday. He was absorbed in choosing another ginger treat.

I returned my attention to the report and read a batch of medical terms that amounted to a verdict of death by strangulation.

"Death by strangulation," I announced. "An obvious conclusion, since they found the body hanging from a tree."

"It doesn't necessarily follow, you know," Creasy began, his mouth full of crumbs.

"Yes, yes, I know. She could have been dead before she was hung." Creasy was fond of disputation; I headed him off.

"Why would you hang a dead person? Why bother? Don't answer," I said hurriedly. "How are you coming with church membership? Is anyone missing?"

"No one," he said, his voice dropping in glum tones. "Not from First Church or Second Church, nor among the Huguenot congregation."

"Perhaps the clothing will tell us something." I spoke in an effort to cheer the man. I picked up the parcel and set it upon a side table.

"They examined the clothing and could find nothing to tell them the identity of the owner," Creasy said.

Even as my fingers touched the string that bound the parcel I reminded myself that I was doing this for the public good. The murderer of the unfortunate woman must not go unpunished. I must be truthful in that I thought myself a better judge of woman's clothing than the sheriff of Salem. I knew I was a far better judge than Mister Increase Cotton. Creasy saw no further than a pretty face, whether she wore rags or a silken gown, he would not notice.

In his own dress, Increase Cotton showed less sense than a scarecrow. He sadly needed a wife to take him in hand, but that task would not fall to me, for which mercy I gave daily thanks to the Lord.

The paper fell away. I reached in with care and unfolded a sturdy gown of striped linen, plain and serviceable, such as any goodwife might wear. Beneath lay a brown petticoat of like quality, a red under petticoat of thin dimity, a pair of red wool stockings, a brown tartan samare or waistcoat and a pair of plain white sleeves with ruffles. Beneath the sleeves I discovered a shift of white lawn, quite new, with a trim of exquisite Flemish lace. I held the cloth to my nose but could get no scent of its owner.

"A pretty thing," Creasy said, eyeing the light garment.

"If the poor woman married on the King's Highway in this she'd be frozen stiff before she got to be a bride," I observed, referring to the custom of evading debts by a smock-marriage.

"No doubt the fiery glances of her swain would keep her warm with blushes," Creasy purred.

"A woman who wears a shift like this is beyond the blushing stage," I said. "That's good Flemish lace." I held the shift up to the light. "London, I'll wager. The lace makers fled to London with the Huguenots," I explained at his look of skepticism. I set the garment back upon the paper and took up the samare for a closer inspection. The woman who wore this bodice was petite in size but she had a full bust; the garment was generous in cut through the bosom. I found a tear at the arm seam which might indicate a struggle, as the garment was well sewn. Next I examined the sleeves. One had a rent at the shoulder and brownish stains speckled the underside. Blood from a scratch or cut, I thought, vowing to test it with a wash of sorrel.

I found no pocket or chain of keys which might give an idea of the woman's identity. By the clothing I thought this was a woman who wanted no notice taken of her, not in public anyway. Neither frill nor ribbon adorned the sleeves, such as a young maid might fancy. This woman's vanity was private. I picked up the shift once more, fingering lace as light as a butterfly's wing. I knew the lady's height, weight and something of her taste from her apparel. Both the coroner and the sheriff had made note of an abundance of golden curls. I thought I knew where I could begin my inquiries.

Shooing Creasy away, I donned my cloak and made for Scarlett's wharf. Sailors have sharp eyes and are great gossips, both qualities of use on board ship. A few inquiries, a flash of coin and I had a name for our victim.

"Arabella Edwards," I told Creasy over dinner, secretly rejoicing when his mouth fell open. A bit of spittle dribbled down his chin. He wiped it hastily with a square of linen.

"How did you find out?" he stammered.

"Oh, I have my methods," I said.

Neither Increase Cotton nor his cousin Cotton Mather could fathom that Hetty Henry, a mere woman, might have resources that they did not. The truth was that through my first husband Jack I knew many seafaring men of high and low station. My second husband, Mister Henry, was a magistrate with a wide acquaintance which included the most important men of our New England colonies. My Jack had brought me wealth in the form of a Spanish prize he'd captured. My Hezekiah Henry taught me how to administer it. I discovered I had a sense for commerce.

"But...but...you've put a name to the woman! Who is she? Where does she come from? Of which church is she a member?"

Creasy set down his fork—a Remarkable Providence, as Cotton Mather would say—ignoring the stuffed eels I'd prepared for him. (I'd boiled the eels in wine and stuffed them with nutmegs and cloves.)

"Eat your pumpkin sauce before it gets cold." I pointed my own fork at his plate.

He glanced down and as quickly looked up at me. "Don't toy with me, Hetty, please. Who is the woman?"

"Arabella Edwards, commonly known as Bella," I answered with satisfaction. "She was Edward Ruckenmaul's mistress. He brought her with him from London but she remained when we sent him back in chains." I referred to the former secretary of the provinces who was arrested with Royal Governor Edmund Andros in the late Rebellion.

"Ruckenmaul's doxy?" Creasy's voice rose to a squeak.

"That's what I heard. Doxy or not, she didn't deserve to die the way she did." I leaned across the table towards him. Secretary Ruckenmaul was loathed by many in the New England colonies including by my companion. Graft, corruption, bribery; these words were synonymous with Edward Ruckenmaul.

"You must not let your dislike of the Secretary taint your search for justice for the woman."

"No...no, of course not. And yet, Ruckenmaul's doxy, Hetty? What kind of immoral woman must she be...have been?"

"I think, sir, that is what we must discover," I said. Noting the flush that crept from his neck to his forehead I added gently, "We don't know her story, Creasy. Men will take advantage of a pretty woman. We don't know how she met her protector or how he seduced her into coming here with him. We only know he abandoned her in a strange wilderness, or so it must have seemed to her. How did she live once he left Boston? Why did she die? These are the questions we must ask."

Creasy lowered his head. He took up his fork and pushed his food around on the plate.

"Eat." I raised my brows and stared at him until he resumed. Let my stuffed eels become cold and congealed? Nonsense.

"There's Indian pudding," I added.

Creasy's face brightened.

We dined in my rooms over my Boston warehouse, rooms I'd kept during my second marriage. I also have a farm in Rumney Marsh.

As I ate, my mind returned to the objects of clothing that were not included in the parcel from the Salem sheriff. Pockets, of course, in which we women carry personal items; a chatelaine's chain of household keys; a hood—she would have worn a hood to cover her hair, especially if she wished to go unnoticed; a cloak if she traveled any distance. The weather was pleasant enough for the samare alone, but nights could be cool. Where was her cloak? How had she traveled to Salem? By carriage? Carriages could be traced. I should have asked more questions down at the wharf. Well, that could be rectified.

Creasy pushed away his dish and leaned back in his chair. "I hope I did justice to your dinner, Hetty. Thank you."

"Justice...." I picked out the word that had most been on my mind. The woman deserved justice, no matter what. I said as much to Creasy.

"Yes," he said simply. "Where do we start? We have a name, thanks to you, but how do we find out about her? There are no friends of Edward Ruckenmaul in Boston."

"No friends maybe, but the merchants were often forced to

do business with him. I will take care of that side of things. How about servants?"

"He did have at least one—Hacker, I think his name was. I met him once."

"I'll leave him to you, then. And King's Chapel—I know you didn't like Mister Ratcliffe, Creasy, but the new chaplain seems a pleasant man, and as the pastor of the Anglican church Mister Myles would know if any of his female members are missing. He might know something of her, of Bella Edwards. You'll have to make inquiries of him." I reached over and placed my hand upon his in a gesture of sympathy. One of the most hurtful grievances against Sir Edward Andros was his usurpation of the South Church for the Anglican services. Good Mister Willard's congregation had to wait out in the rain and the cold until the Anglicans concluded their long services.

While I am certainly of the Reformed faith, I do have commercial ties with many Anglicans in Boston and in London.

Creasy gave me a weak smile. He turned his palm up and grasped my hand, hanging on as if it were a lifeline.

"It will be like old times," I said, referring to several occasions when we had teamed to solve murders at the behest of Cotton Mather. (At least Creasy had been behest; I became involved in spite of the two ministers.)

"Wonderful." His smile vanished. "You mean I'll be thrown into a pond to drown or beaten up and kidnapped on a ship bound for the piratical seas. That's just wonderful."

He removed his hand from mine with a jerk. "What are you getting me into now, Hetty Henry?"

Chapter Three

I walked up a steep hill, stopping twice to catch my breath and relieve a stitch in my side. This was the backside of town, away from the busy wharves and solid houses. Low, spindly shanties of cedar shingles reminded me of the fisherman's cottages at Marblehead. I ignored the mangy dog that barked at my passing and I smiled at the play of dirty children who were damming up a puddle of water with mud canals. So had my own childhood been spent in glorious disregard for cleanliness. In our town we built boats of wood chips with ragged sails rigged to twigs. We would take sticks and stir our little ponds into a frenzy of waves, attempting to swamp our brave vessels in ocean storms.

I stepped around the children, who took no more notice of me than if I had been a fly in the air. Nor were there any adults to be seen. Doors were shut, tiny windows so dirty that a fond mother would not be able to peer out at her urchin's play. Wisps of smoke from crumbling chimneys were the only signs of habitation, even though I knew my passing had not gone unnoticed. Strangers meant trouble to these people. I had not asked Creasy to accompany me to the dwelling of the late Arabella Edwards; compassionate as I knew him to be, ministers meant harangues, scolds, fines and stocks upon this side of the Tri-mountain.

My informant from the wharf directed me to a privet hedge on top of the hill where a rough path led from a gate to the house. There before me stood a neat cottage of cedar shingles with the ell in front, an unusual design for this area. Tucked in between the ell and the front door bloomed a garden of blue iris, gold tansy and leafy yarrow in soft shades of pinks, yellows and whites.

A tiny woman in a black hooded cape popped out of the door.

"Mistress?" Her withered apple face scowled in shortsighted concentration.

I was certain she expected someone else. Arabella Edwards? If so, she had a long wait, poor old woman.

I stepped forward, introducing myself lest she pop back inside the house as quickly as she had appeared.

"My name is Hetty Henry. I am from the Town below. I have news of your mistress. That is, if this is the home of Arabella Edwards."

The little woman drew back a step. Eyes dark as lumps of coal surveyed me before she nodded.

"May I come in? I would be much obliged to you for a cup of water. That's rather a steep hill to climb." I smiled to reassure her that I meant no harm.

The baleful glare she returned me was hardly one of fright. Nonetheless, she beckoned me to follow her into the cottage.

I was quick to follow, stepping into a small entry with a batten door built into the wall to my right. I guessed that this door opened onto a stair to the garret. In front of me lay a spacious parlor. The woman pointed to the fireplace ahead of me before she turned and disappeared.

I walked over to the empty hearth and seated myself on an intricately carved wooden chair. Its twin faced me across the hearth. The floor at my feet gleamed in red oak. Against one wall I noted a handsome gateleg table, sides neatly folded. Upon it I noted a crock filled with cheery orange wood lilies. Two chairs stood near the table as if awaiting tea and gossip.

Flush against the opposite wall sat a green velvet-cushioned bench. The light diffused through two diamond-paned windows above the bench, making the spot quite appropriate for intimate conversation.

I lifted my head to admire a row of glistening pewter plates lined upon the mantle. Tall pewter candlesticks flanked the plates. Wall sconces were ready to add their glow to the room. I admired the effect; the room welcomed visitors with its soft, comfortable appearance.

The old woman returned with a pewter tankard in her hand, which I accepted with gratitude. The water tasted cool and sweet to my parched throat. The coal eyes watched me with every swallow.

"Thank you," I said, handing her the empty tankard. "I'm afraid I am the bearer of sad news. It concerns your mistress." *This is awkward*, I thought. I had not counted upon having to break the news of Arabella Edward's tragic end. I clasped my hands in my lap and forced myself to face the little woman in the black cape who stood before me, waiting.

"Arabella Edwards is dead."

The old woman received the news with astonishing calm. "By what means?" she asked. Her eyes narrowed, assessing me. Whether for the truth of my words or for my character I did not know.

"She was found hanging from the Salem gallows, but not of her own doing, nor of the courts, please be assured of that," I said. "She did not kill herself."

"No, she would not do that."

The old woman just stood there, frowning, but I did not think she was frowning at me. Finally I gestured to the chair on the other side of the hearth. I wished the fire were lit, to provide some warmth for the poor woman at my hard news.

"Please," I said, "won't you be seated? I would like to ask you some questions, if I may."

The old woman's brows rose at my impertinence but she turned and marched to the chair and plunked herself down. Then she nodded her head, which I took to mean her assent to my questions. I felt she should know by what authority I acted.

"I have been asked to assist Mister Increase Cotton of the

Summer Street Church with inquiries regarding the death of your late mistress, Arabella Edwards. It was murder, and her murder will not go unpunished, I assure you. We will have justice done here."

I went on, ignoring a skeptical look from the woman. "Mister Cotton and I have had some success in these cases. We were asked by Mister Cotton Mather to look into Mistress Edwards' death, as it is thought the answer lies here in Boston, rather than in Salem town. She was not known there at all."

Perhaps it was the mention of Cotton Mather's name that relaxed the rigid old back—Cousin Cotton has that effect upon elderly females. She crooked a finger at me, signing that I should continue. I felt as if I were back in Dame School.

"Ummm," I hesitated, gathering my thoughts. "If you would answer a few questions about your mistress..." I left the suggestion hanging in the air, looking at her withered face to ascertain the extent of the cooperation I was likely to receive. I just as quickly looked down at my thumbs. "It is to find the fiend who murdered her, you know." I spoke in a defensive tone. These people did not like to speak to strangers.

"Perhaps you should start by asking my name."

The tart suggestion took me off guard. "Ummm, yes," I agreed. "What is it?"

"I am Esther Thripenny, servant to Mistress Arabella Edwards."

Esther Thripenny sat with composure, waiting for my next question. I marveled at her self-command, considering the sad news I brought. But then the aged often take death for granted.

"Did you come over from England with your mistress?" I asked.

"No."

Although this answer was to the point, I encouraged her with a nod of my head to expand upon the point.

"My mistress hired me in Town to move up here with her. I cook and clean and act as companion to her."

"Did you know her before you moved here, when she was

the...friend of Secretary Ruckenmaul?"

"I did some sewing and mending for her but I cannot say that I knew the woman well. Do you know the lady who sews for you?"

I bridled at the challenge in her voice. "I sew for myself," I said. I was not about to explain my life to her. "Presumably you got to learn more about your mistress living in close proximity to her for...how many years? How long has she lived in this house?"

"Three years."

"Since we shipped the secretary in chains back to London, then?"

"Yes," she answered.

I took private satisfaction in that event. Edward Ruckenmaul was even more hated in New England than his tyrant of a master, the former Royal Governor Edmund Andros. Both men were tried in London on our charges of graft and corruption, but a London jury found more tolerance for their behavior than a Bay Colony jury would have. More's the pity.

Arabella Edwards must have found this cottage quite a comedown from the secretary's mansion in town.

"When did you last see your mistress?" I asked. "Did she tell you where she was going? With whom did she go?" I fired these questions at the old woman, hoping to jolt her into more responsive answers.

Mistress Thripenny's composure remained un-shattered, however.

"She left here seven days ago, for Salem, to see the witches. She did not tell me with whom she meant to travel. I cannot tell you that. My mistress treasured discretion above all, and was valued by her friends for that quality." Esther Thripenny gazed at me if as I was deficient in that particular trait.

"A necessary quality in her profession," I noted with some dryness. Yet that very quality of discretion would make it more difficult to capture her killer. If she had only confided in her elderly companion I would have a name for the constable.

"Why would she want to see the witches?" I asked, pressing for any knowledge of the victim's habits. "Was she fearful of them? Did she have an acquaintance among the accused? What was her mood when you last saw her?"

"My mistress was of a naturally cheerful disposition," Esther said. "As for her reason for wanting to see the witches, why it seems that everyone is desirous of seeing them. Are you not curious yourself to view the strange antics of the poor girls who are the victims of these vile creatures?"

I shook my head, having been too occupied by business to undertake a trip to Salem from mere curiosity. At least I had learned from this old woman that Bella Edwards had gone willingly to Salem. She did not expect to die there, which meant she had trusted someone.

"Did she often go off on trips like this?"

"Sometimes..., but not often. And she was never gone for more than two nights," the old woman said.

I felt pleased that she offered me this tidbit of information.

"Did she go with a man?"

"My mistress has many friends, both male and female. She is a welcome guest in many homes of consequence in Boston. Sometimes she would tell me where she was going, sometimes not. It was not my place to ask." The old spine stiffened as hard as the chair in which she sat.

"No, I meant a particular man with whom she kept company...like Secretary Ruckenmaul. Since he is no longer her protector, is there a particular man whose company she favors? Favored..." I corrected myself. The woman was the whore of a corrupt, detested government official, yet I hesitated to name her as such before this tiny bird-like old woman. Perhaps I feared having my knuckles whacked with a birch rod as in school.

Esther Thripenny merely frowned at me. "There are many men who admire my mistress. She is...was...very beautiful and a lively, good-natured young woman. I know what they say of her in town, but she knew how to conduct herself in the finest company. She was generous, loyal and kind. Nor did I ever hear one complaint from her lips when she moved from a fine house in Boston to this poor hill."

I glanced around the room. Arabella Edwards had good taste in furnishings. Many items in the room I thought had come from London. "This is a very comfortable house," I remarked.

"She made it so." The old woman snapped at me sharp as a coachman's whip.

I felt defensive. "If I don't ask these questions, the constable will."

"John Phillymort?" She sniffed. "The man's a pompous know-it-all. Always was. I've known him since he was a snotty-nosed brat."

I could not argue with her assessment of the Boston constable. I was too young to have known Phillymort as a child, but I could well imagine him as the tattler who ran and squealed on his playfellows at the least harmless frolic.

I leaned forward in my chair. This was the most important question. "If you would tell me the names of her friends—" I began.

"I cannot."

I frowned at her reticence. "Discretion is all well and good, Mistress Thripenny, but you must remember that your mistress has been murdered! Your cooperation is needed if we are to discover her killer."

"I cannot," she repeated, her voice calm. "My mistress never introduced me to her friends, nor did she name them to me. She had silly names for them all, like Badbones or Cattails or Madame Beaver—that is how I knew them."

Well, then, a description of them—height, color of hair, eyes, manner of dress...whatever you can remember," I urged.

The old woman shook her head. "I rise early and take an early supper before I retire to my bed upstairs. I'm the one tends to the fires, the baking, the cooking, the sewing, washes the linens...she has a lad to help with the heavy lifting and chopping wood and such. He's a simpleton, a neighbor's boy, and you have to stand over him to see it gets done right, that one." She clicked her tongue. "I go to my bed to sleep, not to spy on my mistress' company." Esther Thripenny's black, beady eyes regarded me with disdain.

I felt that I had reached an impasse here. My shoulders slumped. I'd hoped to astonish Creasy with my discoveries. Perhaps I thought I could solve the murder without his help. So much for my vanity. I stood up to take my leave.

Chapter Four

I would not have noticed the man except for the street urchins who were now throwing stones at their mud dykes. A great deal of the pleasure in building these structures is in destroying them. As I passed, a muddy missile came dangerously close to my skirts. I turned to chastise the little imps when a sudden movement caught my eye. A man in a tea-colored cloak ducked behind a tree. Unfortunately the man's broad frame didn't fit. One shoulder, a hunk of cloak and a hat brim remained in my sight.

I walked briskly on my way—much easier going down than walking up, after all. About halfway down the hill I pretended a misstep and glanced quickly behind me. The man in the tea cloak hung back. At the foot of the hill I turned right. The man followed. He turned on to the Corn Hill, as did I. He walked down Water Street behind me. I led him to the wharves where I determined to lose him. Lead him to my warehouse rooms I would not. If he did not know who I was, I would not help him find out.

I stepped into the chandler's shop and was greeted by the owner with a cheerful hail.

"Mister Jones," I smiled. "I am very well, thank you, except for a bit of bother. I wonder if I might trouble you for a favor." I moved across the floor towards the man.

The chandler's eyes narrowed. He cocked a graying head.

"There is a man who followed me down from the Tri-mountain. He has a tea-colored cloak and a broad frame with a beaver hat. I'd rather he didn't find out where I live," I explained. As I spoke I fingered a row of long white candles. "I'll take a dozen of these, if you please."

The chandler reached under the counter for a sheet of wrapping paper. "I'll see to it, Mrs. Henry." He winked. "Just you excuse me for a moment, madam."

He disappeared through a door behind him, the wrapping paper fluttering in his hand.

I wandered through the shop, eyeing the goods displayed on tables and counters. There were candles of tallow, bayberry, beeswax; holders of pewter and brass in a variety of styles; lanterns of tin and of brass; wall sconces of tin and glass. If my gentleman spy bothered to look through the shop window, he would see no more than a woman considering some goods to purchase.

After a brief time Mr. Jonas returned with a twine-wrapped parcel, which parcel he handed to me. "All taken care of, Mrs. Henry," he said and winked. "Now just you wait another moment and I'll have my lad carry this for you. He's a sharp boy, is our Jeremy. Did they like the oysters in that New York Colony you went to?"

I nodded. "They do like their oysters in Albany," I said.

"Well, we've got 'em to spare. Good oysters. Can't see why you loaded the Anhinga with all them shells, though," he said, scratching his head. "Peculiar people, I guess."

"The local natives make jewelry of them." I declined to go into detail about my new business venture, which was the manufacture of wampompeague or *sewant* as the Dutch in Albany called it. I expected this to turn into a lucrative sideline for me.

"Oh, the heathen savages." Jonas spoke in a dismissive tone, as if the Albany Indians were of little account.

I could have told him that the Albany Indians were the only things standing between him and the French in Canada but I curbed my impatience. Boston people were more afraid of the Canadian priests grabbing their souls than of the hatchets of their allies, the Eastern Indians.

Jonas turned. "Ah, there's my youngest now," he said.

A small lad in an oversized shirt and wide-legged trousers swaggered in from the hall. I judged him to be about ten years of age. He had a thatch of brown hair and alert green eyes. I liked the look of him.

"Ready to go, sir." The lad saluted Mr. Jonas.

"This is Mrs. Henry, Jeremy. You are to carry a parcel for her to her home. You understand me?" Jonas searched the boy's face.

The boy nodded. He turned to me with a quick grin. "I'll see you home safe, lady."

I handed my parcel to my guardian.

Jeremy set a brisk pace. We walked for two blocks before two burly men stumbled out of an alley. They appeared to be inebriated, but one of them pulled off his cap at my passing and the other gave my little protector a civil nod. They lumbered on down the street.

Scarcely one moment later I turned at a sudden cry. Jeremy stopped by my side. The two burly men were bending over a man in a tea-colored cloak who lay flat upon his back in the middle of the street. The boy and I watched as the burly men pulled the fellow up by his arms, apologizing in loud tones as they brushed him off with clumsy hands.

"Sorry, sir...didn't mean to bump you," said the man with the cap, his words slurred.

"Come...no harm done, I hope. Buy you a drink, shall we?" said the other.

A ragged arm fell over the poor gentleman's shoulder while the man with the cap grasped him in a friendly bear hug. "Have a little r...rum." The gentleman in his tea cloak was bundled off down the street, a street that was filled with welcoming taverns.

Jeremy grinned up at me, his fox-green eyes dancing. He took my arm and with great self-possession for such a young man, and escorted me to my home.

Increase Cotton upbraided me for my heedless behavior

when I told him of my venture on the Tri-Mountain.

"In the future, Hetty, if you do not trust me enough to include me, please see that you take along one of your hearty laborers or sailors when you go out. This man has murdered one woman in a most brutal fashion. If you go about asking questions about her it could be dangerous. The fact that you were followed like that makes me nervous."

"Nonsense," I huffed. "This is Boston. If I can't walk about the streets of Boston I might as well turn Papist and join a nunnery."

Creasy's aristocratic nose wrinkled in distaste at my threat.

"I am serious, Hetty."

I changed the subject. "Did you speak with the Anglican minister?"

He slouched in his chair. "Yes, to no effect. He doesn't recall the woman, though he's only served their church a brief time. He seems to be making a real effort to know his people. He was shocked by the murder of the young woman—he promised to ask his members for any information they might have about her. I have to say, I thought him an amiable fellow."

This he confessed in a grudging tone. The former Royal Governor Andros had confiscated a Reformed Church for his long Anglican services, causing much rancor. Poor old Mister Willard's congregation was left out in the cold and rain. Perhaps the new minister could smooth ruffled feathers. He'd certainly made a start with Creasy, although I must admit Increase Cotton is more tolerant of other people's worship than many of his colleagues.

"Let's hope he finds someone who knows the woman. I certainly failed to learn anything much from the old servant." I had to admit my failure.

"I may have more luck with her," Creasy said. "Esther Thripenny—I've heard that name. I think I'll pay a visit to the Tri-mountain myself, if you don't mind, Hetty."

I shrugged. "The only reason I didn't ask you to come with me is that the people up there might balk at talking to a minister. They are most often cursed and scolded for their sins by the clergy. Not that poverty or drunkenness is an excuse for sinning," I added.

"I don't condemn my congregation, Hetty, and they are quite as poor as the souls upon the Tri-mountain." Creasy scrunched up his mouth.

I patted his coat sleeve to pacify him. "I know you don't," I said. "The only one you're in the habit of cursing and condemning is me. Do you remember when you accused me of being a witch?"

Creasy's face reddened. "But...but...I admitted I was wrong, Hetty. I apologized for that. I didn't really know you then."

I could not help giggling. "I remember how you apologized. It was most effective."

The young minister's face flushed even brighter.

I took pity upon him. "I hope you have better luck with the old woman than I did," I said. "In the meantime I'll return to the chandler shop and find out the name of my spy. I'm sure they uncovered his name."

"Not without me, you're not. I mean it, Hetty. You're not to go about asking questions by yourself." He folded his arms and leaned back in his chair, his face grim as the clouds of a gathering thunder storm.

There is no use arguing with the man when he digs in his heels, as I'd come to know.

"Fine. We'll go together," I said.

"Fine. When? It's late now."

"Tomorrow morning, after breakfast. No, wait...meet me at the chandler's before breakfast. We'll get the name and then go to Milk's Tavern to eat. Mrs. Milk serves a fine fish with pumpkin sauce. She'll give us a quiet corner and we can plan our next move. Is that agreeable?"

"Perfectly." He unfolded his long form and rose from the seat. "I'll have the afternoon to work on my sermon."

I rose with him. "Oh, and what is the topic to be?"

"I thought to draw from the book of Esther, oddly enough.

There the wicked cease from troubling, and there the weary be at rest."
    "Arabella Edwards will be at rest when justice is done her."
    It was my turn to feel grim.

Chapter Five

The man who followed me down the Tri-mountain was named Ephrata Phinny. I stopped by the chandler's shop to obtain the name on my way to meet Creasy at Milk's Tavern. Over a hearty breakfast we decided that we should find out more about Mr. Phinny before we tackled him. Phinny kept a shop on King Street and was known to be a supporter of the former Royal Governor and a member of the Anglican Church.

We agreed to pay a morning visit to Esther Thripenny.

"Prying information from her will be like tearing open raw oysters with your fingers," I said.

"Perhaps she will prove more amenable to a man's presence. I have a way with elderly females." Creasy spoke with a serious mien.

It's a good thing he liked the elderly, I thought to myself, *because he certainly managed to aggravate women of his own age.*

After our meal we set out to climb the Tri-mountain. I soon found myself puffing to keep up with my companion. He leaned into the hill like a lanky mountain goat.

"What's the haste?" I managed to call out.

The gentleman merely grunted at me, so I saved my breath for the rest of the climb. Today there were no signs of the urchins. One hoped that they would be in dame school, but the sad reality was that they were probably still asleep upon their cots. The Town must be reminded of its duty to these children. I resolved to see to it.

We reached the hedge and turned in the break to see the house. I noted with approval that the shutters were closed and draped in black. Esther Thripenny paid the proper respect to her deceased mistress. As I turned to say as much to Creasy, he called out a greeting.

"Good morning, mistress."

Esther Thripenny stood in the doorway, a grim little figure in a dress of dove gray. She welcomed us in a grave manner, although I noted a tremor in one hand.

"Mrs. Henry," she said, her head held in a regal lift.

I began to introduce her to my companion but she interrupted me.

"I know who you are, sir," she said, reaching out to take Creasy's hand. "Mister Increase Cotton is welcome at any time."

Her brow lifted and a thin smile stretched her skin.

She kept his hand in hers and practically dragged him inside the house. I followed before she could shut the door upon me.

"Mister Cotton, you are the answer to a poor widow's prayer. I am sorely in need of a wise masculine presence to guide me."

Creasy folded his body in half in an attempt at a bow. He loomed over her.

"I shall assist you in any way I can, Mistress Thripenny. I shall be pleased to do so."

"Oh, sir, I know I may depend upon you! How your kind words lighten my load!"

The wrinkled face wrinkled into a simper that was dreadful to behold. Perhaps Creasy did have a way with the elderly. Esther Thripenny grabbed his coat sleeve and held on as she led him into the parlor. I was ignored. Sometimes it is invaluable to be ignored; I have picked up many valuable scraps of information by that method—usually when doing business with men of commerce.

The mantle above the hearth was draped in black cloth.

Black cloth covered pictures and mirrors. Yet there was a fire in the hearth which made the room seem cheery enough.

Esther Thripenny insisted that Creasy take the chair next to the hearth while she seated herself opposite him. I took a seat upon a bench next to the wall.

What a difference the fire makes, I thought, recalling my prior visit. I watched the orange and blue flames race across a stout log. Charred sticks lay in black and velvet tangles at the log's base. This fire had been set long prior to our visit; she could not have known we were coming. "Why was a fire set in the best parlor?" I wondered.

"You have suffered a great loss." Creasy offered his condolences in an unctuous voice.

"Sir, we have been robbed." The old woman shook her hands in agitation.

Creasy nodded in understanding. "A young woman, taken in the prime of her life...her promise has been lost to us."

"I say we have been robbed, sir."

"Ah yes, we lose our belief in the goodness of mankind in such tragic circumstances...we are robbed of our innocence, in a manner of speaking. Yet we must not lose our faith in God's justice, no matter how foul the crime. Indeed, I have come to pray with you that justice may be granted to us, on earth as surely as there will be Eternal Justice dispensed by the Almighty Judge. Oh, this villain will pay for his wickedness, please be assured of it, mistress. Do not succumb to despair..."

"Oh, sir, I have not lost my faith in Divine Justice and I will gladly pray with you for the Redemption of my poor mistress, but I tell you again that we have been robbed!"

"What taken?" I interrupted, leaning forward on my bench. Creasy had not the slightest notion of the woman's meaning.

Esther Thripenny turned to me in relief.

"The only thing I have found missing is the accounts book—to my knowledge, that is. I have been searching the house but I cannot see that anything else is gone." She turned to Creasy again.

"What am I to do, sir? It seems a strange thing to steal, is it not?"

"The accounts book..." I tapped the bench with my fingertips. I could think of several reasons to steal an accounts book. There were many of my rivals in commerce who would like to steal my accounts books, I was sure of that. "Was the woman in some sort of partnership with anyone? Since Secretary Ruckenmaul, I mean. What kind of accounts did she keep?"

"Why, the household accounts. I know of no other kind." Esther Thripenny frowned in thought.

"Did you see the entries in the accounts book?" I asked.

"Why yes, I often made entries myself...when she was away from home and I made purchases of food or cloth or laces. She always provided for any purchases I might have to make when she was away. And of course, I continued to sew for her and to make her dresses. She did love to have well made clothing upon her person, poor lady. Oh, she was not vain—you must not think that of her. Yet she dressed with care, as is proper, don't you think?" Esther Thripenny appealed to Creasy.

"Indeed, I do think it proper in a woman to dress with care for her person," he agreed. "I do not deem that vanity in a woman."

"Oh, I am glad that you understand, Mister Cotton. I have heard that you were a man of understanding."

The minister basked in her praise like a sunflower to the sun.

"And you are certain there were no entries but of a household nature? You saw the entries she made in her own handwriting?" I felt obliged to persist in my questioning, now that she was so forthcoming in Creasy's presence. A man of understanding indeed!

"Oh, I had full access to the accounts, I assure you. There was nothing there but plain household matters. I often watched her make entries—we sat in the kitchen of a morning, at least once a week after our breakfast, and she would sit at the table and tally up our bills and set aside a sum of money to pay the tradesmen and enter each transaction upon the page. The poor lady!"

Tears clouded the old eyes. I felt obliged to offer to go into the kitchen and make a cup of tea for her.

At her nod, I took myself off. There were more questions I longed to ask but they must wait. I knew that Creasy was versed in soothing those who grieved for a lost one.

The kitchen was well provisioned with a large hearth and kettles and spits and skillets of every size. There was a large cupboard groaning under a display of shining pewter and glistening glassware. On a table near the kitchen door I found a small wooden chest upon which was painted *simples* in an elegant scroll. I rummaged through the contents but could find no India tea there so I opened a bottle of Hyperion leaves and made up an infusion.

I assembled cups of steaming brew, which I carried into the parlor.

Esther Thripenny took hers with a sigh. "Oh dear, I have not had time to bake the funeral cakes, what with the robbery and checking the household..."

"Don't fret about it," I advised her. "I'll send to Town for some."

"It doesn't seem right, somehow," she said, shaking her head. "I should have baked them, just the same. It doesn't seem right. Why, I have nothing to offer you, and what of the others who come to offer their respects? What will I have to serve them?" The old woman began to rise from her seat.

Creasy waved her down. "Now, now, mistress. Seat yourself! You've had a heavy load laid upon your shoulders. Let us share the burden. Mrs. Henry will see that you have funeral cakes to serve; just leave that in her capable hands."

I passed a cup of the Hyperion tea to Creasy. "Ask her how she discovered the accounts book was missing." I whispered this to him before seating myself upon the bench with my own cup, warming my hands on the round bowl. I inhaled the fragrant sweet scent of raspberry.

"Now Mistress Thripenny, just you rest for a moment.

Enjoy your cup of tea. When you are quite ready, why don't you tell us what happened?" Creasy spoke in a soothing tone.

Esther Thripenny sipped from her cup in careful deliberation.

"When did you discover the house had been robbed?" I asked, unable to contain myself.

Creasy gave me a glance of reproach. "When you are ready, mistress..." Creasy crooned to the old woman in a voice like maple syrup.

I forced myself to remain silent while Mistress Esther sipped, and sipped, and sipped again. Finally she lowered her cup, setting it carefully upon a small round table.

"I rose as usual, sir..." she began, her eyes on the young minister. "At first I didn't find anything amiss. In the kitchen I went to light the fire which I had banked the evening before. I took a cup of broth and a slice of bread for my breakfast. I never take a large breakfast but my poor mistress enjoyed a substantial meal. Baked eggs, slices of ham and chunks of boiled vegetables. Anyway, after I ate I went into her bedroom to air out the sheets—I don't care, my poor mistress may be dead and gone but I will keep her bedclothes aired—and I noticed a paper sticking out of her desk. I thought it strange, for I was certain I hadn't seen it there or I should have put it away where it belongs." She clasped her hands, eyeing Creasy as if she dreaded his censure. That gentleman was all benevolence, however.

"I opened the desk," she continued, "and the paper fell out. It was a bill from a tradesman. That reminded me it was her day to do the accounts and I thought I would take out the accounts books later in the morning. I looked into the desk but could not tell whether there was anything amiss. The papers seemed to be in proper order except for this one bill. I placed it in a cubby and shut the desk. From my position I noted that one of the bed curtains was lifted up by the hem and tucked beneath the mattress. Well that wouldn't do; I wouldn't leave the curtains any way but hanging proper. So I went over to straighten it, and that's when I discovered one of the pillows askew!" Esther Thripenny crossed her chest with both hands, her face registering horror.

Creasy made a sympathetic hum, encouraging her to proceed.

Would that she was as talkative with me, I thought. With effort, I kept my expression of sympathy.

"I know that I have been upset, Mister Cotton, what with my mistress being killed and such, but those pillows were plumped and set just as they should be, and I know that. If my mistress should walk into the door this very moment her pillows would be plumped and set just so. Now who would move my dear dead mistress's pillow? Who would do such a thing?" The old eyes darkened with indignation. She shook her head at the incomprehensible evil of mankind.

Neither Creasy nor I could enlighten her.

"I went back to the kitchen to make myself an infusion of comfrey...this Hyperion tea is all well and good but comfrey is best for nerves." Esther Thripenny glanced in my direction before she turned her attention back to the minister.

"That's when I began to look around and notice little things out of place. The door to the cupboard was slightly ajar, a skillet moved out of place...I went to the cupboard to the draw for the accounts book—she kept the accounts book in the kitchen because that's where she worked on the accounts, you know—and the accounts book was missing! Gone! No sign of it anywhere! Well, I didn't know what to do. Maybe I was going queer in the head, I thought, but then queer in the head or not, I wouldn't have mussed her bed—that I would not do."

"And nothing else is missing?" Creasy asked, bestirring himself.

Esther shook her gray head. "I looked all over the house, I did, and nothing else gone missing except for the accounts book. Isn't that odd? That's why I am thankful for your visit, Mister Cotton. You will know what to do."

I could have corrected her of the notion, but I, being a mere woman, would not have been heard.

Chapter Six

Creasy and I spoke at the same time. I began, "Madam, have you seen any strangers...?"

Creasy leaned forward, gazing at Esther Thripenny with concern. "Mistress, do you have someone who can come and stay with you? I don't think you should remain in this house by yourself. A relative...a neighbor...a friend, perhaps?"

Esther Thripenny thought for a moment. "There's my neighbor's boy, Abel, the one chops and carries the wood for me, but he's less than useless—a great, hulking coward of a boy." She tapped the side of her head with one finger. "He's simple in his mind, you know."

"Can he make a noise?" Creasy asked. "If someone were to attempt another search, could he cry out and call for help?"

Esther nodded. "Oh yes, he can howl like a wolf when he's hit, I assure you. You can hear him down in your church in town, the great blubbering baby. And I only give him a tap with a little stick when he drops a log on my clean floor or breaks my footstool by tripping over it, the clumsy clod."

"That's all we need, then, someone who can give a warning. Perhaps you could find a place for him for the night. Bar your doors as well, mistress," Creasy warned.

"Oh, I do that, Mister Cotton. I don't know how the person got inside. It's a good thing I had the bar set on the door to the stairs, there." She motioned with her hand. "That's where I sleep, up there. 'Twas my mistress who bade me bar the door when I went upstairs to my bed. She said as how one of her guests might wander where he shouldn't be if he'd imbibed too much. Not that it ever happened, but she was that concerned for me. Oh, poor Arabella! How kind a mistress!" The old woman pulled a square of linen from her apron and dabbed at her eyes. "Such a sweet lady...so thoughtful..."

I wanted to put some questions to the woman but Creasy held a finger to his lips, motioning me to be silent. He made sympathetic noises at the woman.

After several moments, he turned to me. "Hetty, will you make arrangements for this boy to come stay with Mistress Thripenny. Make sure his family understands the situation. The more neighbors who keep a look-out, the less we shall have to worry."

Worry? I wasn't worried in the least. Personally, I thought the old lady was tough as nails. She was reveling in the attentions of the young minister. I rose from my seat in obedience. I did not even argue.

"Oh, and Hetty, make certain the lad knows that all he has to do is to cry out in a loud voice. He is not to attempt to fight the thief."

Esther Thripenny snorted into her handkerchief.

Since I was not allowed to question the old woman, I might as well question the neighbors, I thought. I let myself out the front door.

Sounds from the back brought me around the ell to the woodpile. A tall young man chopped pieces of log for firewood. I watched him work, unobserved. The young man was intent upon his chopping. The lad had strong arms and broad shoulders on a lanky frame. He had a long face with a long jaw, a wide mouth and a full head of brown hair drawn back and tied with a black ribbon. A frown of concentration marred an otherwise pleasant countenance. He set down the axe and wiped his sweaty forehead.

"Good morning," I addressed him as I stepped across the lawn.

"Good morning." He spoke with a polite smile, exposing

good strong teeth. His eyes were soft brown and as trusting as a puppy.

"Are you Abel? My name is Hetty Henry."

Abel took my outthrust hand and pumped it up and down. "I am Abel," he said. "Pleased to meet you, Hetty Henry." The young man folded his body into a gallant bow. He straightened. "My name is Abel Keyne."

"Abel Keyne, I am here to help Mistress Thripenny.

"I help Mistress Thripenny, too," he said, motioning to the cut wood. "I chop and stack the wood and carry it in for Mistress. She pays me. I stack it neat. No loose sticks laying around for a body to trip over." He parroted the words in an unconscious imitation of Esther Thripenny.

"That's very good, Abel. You do good work."

"I have to get this wood stacked now." He pointed to the sticks at his feet.

"Just a moment, Abel, if you please. Mistress Thripenny needs your help. Would you like to get paid some extra coins?"

"Oh, she won't pay me any more money, Hetty Henry. She says I'm nor worth another penny." The long brow furrowed. "Do you best, that's all the Lord asks of us, my mother says. Do your best, Abel."

"Why that's so," I replied. "I think you do very good work, and I shall pay you for it, not Mistress Thripenny. You don't have to worry about that, Abel. Do you know Mistress Edwards that lived here?" I was curious.

"Mistress Edwards is dead. My mother says she's living with the Lord now. Tom says she's laying with the Devil but I don't see why she would do that. The Devil is a bad man. Mistress Edwards is a nice lady. She's pretty. She gives me a new penny when she sees me, and I don't even have to work for it. She's a nice lady."

A bright smile lit Abel's face.

"Yes, well Mistress Edwards is dead now, Abel, but I shall give you ten new pennies a night if you will stay here and keep Mistress Thripenny company for a few nights. Mistress

Thripenny will put up a cot for you. You are to sleep in the house and to make a great deal of noise if a bad man tries to break inside. Do you think you can do that? Cry out for help really loud?"

Abel nodded. "I can make a loud noise. Mistress Thripenny says I make too much noise. I don't think she will let me sleep here. I sleep on my own cot at home." He reached down and lifted a large stick of wood from the ground.

"Mistress Thripenny needs our help, Abel," I reminded him. "A bad man broke into the house last night. She won't mind if you sleep on a cot in the kitchen. We need someone who can make a great deal of noise if this bad man tries to break in again. I will pay you ten new pennies a night, for every night you are asked to sleep here." Abel knew how to bargain, I thought.

"You have to ask my mother if I can sleep here," Abel said. He bent over and picked up another large hunk of wood. "And I can't have ten new pennies. My mother says I might lose them if I have more than one." A drop of spittle ran down the corner of his mouth.

"What if I give nine pennies to your mother and give you one new penny a day? Would that be all right?" I smiled at him.

Abel beamed. "That would be all right. One new penny— my mother puts them in a bottle for me. When I have enough in the bottle I may go to the shops and buy a new wool cap."

"Oh, that will be nice, Abel," I said. "What color cap shall you choose?"

"Red!" There was no hesitation.

"That's a fine color, Abel. Now, shall we just step over to see your mother?"

Abel shook his head. "I have to stack this wood. No loose sticks laying around for a body to trip over."

"That's right, I said, patting his shoulder. Would that the other lads in town had Abel's devotion to duty! "You go on with your work. I'll go speak with your mother and ask her for permission for you to sleep here for a few nights. Where do you live?"

Abel pointed to an untrimmed jumble of privet that divided the two properties. "Just over the hedge, Hetty Henry," he said.

I left him at his work, scooping up a pile of wood and carrying it to the woodpile. I followed the scraggly branches until I found a break. Stepping through the privet I discovered a small hovel set back from the road. The roof leaned to one side, the shakes were ragged and missing in places, but I noticed the window was clear and clean of dirt. A person could actually see through it.

My insistent knock was answered by a woman in a shabby russet gown and a patched apron. The apron was clean except for a few green stains. From the doorway I could see bunches of herbs hung to dry from the rafters. A peppery scent of thyme and pennyroyal permeated the air.

"Good morning, madam. My name is Hetty Henry," I said, extending my hand. "Are you Mistress Keyne, Abel's mother?"

The woman barred the doorway, ignoring my hand. "Missus Keyne," she muttered.

I explained my errand and the need for kind neighbors to keep watch on the house of Arabella Edwards.

Mrs. Keyne sniffed at the name. She sniffed again at the plight of Esther Thripenny. But she held out her hand for the coins I brought out from my pocket. She nodded when I asked whether her son could spend several nights in the Edwards house and nodded again when I asked her whether her son was capable of raising an alarm in case of an intruder.

"Indeed," I added, "I find the lad a most capable young man—very apt and very able."

The woman stepped back and slammed the door in my face.

Well, I reflected, there are some people who do not appreciate a good pun.

I walked to the road and tried to summon someone to the door of the shack across the way from the Keynes. No one answered my summons. Two other doors remained barred to me, although I could hear distinct sounds coming from both.

41

Working my way down the hill, I finally had better luck. A dirty-faced urchin responded to my persistent banging.

"Whaddayawan?"

I interpreted the snarl as an inquiry as to my business. "Is your mother home, boy?"

Tiny faces with beady eyes peered from the dark behind the boy's back.

"She's workin'"

I heard whispering behind the door, like the rustling of leaves on a lonely road.

"When will she be home?" I asked, as civil as I could be.

Titterings tiny as the feet of field mice sounded behind the door.

"She's workin," the boy repeated, thin brows formed into a fierce scowl.

Behind the door a high-pitched squeal was abruptly cut off.

"Are you the man of the house?" I asked, trying to ingratiate myself with the surly urchin.

"Whaddayawan?" The demand came out in a would-be bellow.

I had an inspiration. "Why, I am looking for smart lads to join His Majesty's Young Spies Training League, Boston Company. They listen and inform on Papist plots or possible Indian raids or robbers or murders and such and then they report back to the secret chief. I can't tell you who that is, because that is a secret, but I am his sergeant, Sergeant Henry, and you would report to me...if you join us."

At the urchin's look of skepticism I improvised. "You see, people don't expect a woman to recruit spies, so this is an effective disguise. Did I say the pay is one shilling when you join and two shillings for every plot you discover or lawbreaker you unearth?" I reached into my pocket and produced a coin, which I waved about in the air, just out of reach of grubby paws. "It's like taking the King's shilling, like soldiers do. I wanted to ask your mother if she knew of any likely lads for the Boston Company, but I can see that you would make a fine young spy."

I mentally asked for forgiveness for my exaggerations, but in effect I *was* recruiting spies. Creasy did not need to know about my efforts or the means I employed to obtain information. We both worked for the same cause: justice.

The beady little rodent eyes glittered at sight of the coin. "I'll join. Gimme the shilling." The lad stuck out a thin, dirty hand.

"Me too, me too, me too!" A chorus of voices rose from the door frame; tiny paws shot out from the black void.

The urchin pushed back the paws with ruthless determination.

"Not so fast," I said, hedging. "You have to pass the test first." I slid the coin back into my pocket.

Greedy eyes watched the coin disappear; a soft collective sigh wafted from behind the door. I began to feel uneasy.

"What do I got to do?" The urchin spoke in a world-weary tone that belied his years, which I judged at nine or ten. How young to learn that betrayal comes at a price!

"Answer some questions, that's all, and if you pass you'll get your first pay. And your first assignment." Creasy did say we needed neighborhood eyes.

"Do you know the lady who lives behind the big hedge on the hill?" I pointed.

"You mean Bella the Whore of Babylon? That's in the Bible," he said at the shock that must have registered upon my face. "She was hung for a witch, that one...is that the case we're to work on?"

I collected myself. "Yes, that's the case, and she wasn't hung for a witch. She was hung by a bad man." If there really was a Young Spies Training League, this one was ripe for recruitment. "Did you ever see a gentleman go to Mistress Edward's house?"

The lad snorted. "One gentleman? I seen loads of gentlemen go to Bella's. She was a whore, you know. Oh, she wore fine duds, but my ma didn't like her. Thought she was too good for us. Ma would've liked her leftovers, though."

"The men?" I asked, puzzled and horrified at the same time.

"The duds. Bella's gentlemen wouldn't look at my ma. She ain't pretty or nothin'." The urchin made this observation in a matter of fact manner.

"Would you recognize any of these men if you saw them again?" Hope began to stir within me. The lad was sharp as a sailor's needle.

"Didn't see their faces," he said.

My hope sank.

"Some come in coaches, some on horseback. I'd know them horses." The lad was quite positive in tone.

"Would you?" My voice rose in a squeak. Who knew that help would come in such a small, surly form?

The lad gave his head an emphatic shake. "Big black with a white star—skittish, that one—comes on Mondays. Tuesdays is a neat brown trotter. The man sort of dressed like the horse, plain and neat. Then there was a coach on Thursdays with a matched pair of greys—big ones with hairy hoofs. You know the kind?"

I nodded.

"Then a big man on Fridays on a reddish horse. That one looks strong and fast. I bet the black and the reddish one would make a fine race of it. I think the reddish one would win, though. Black star is more showy. Don't think he has the stamina." At this pronouncement the urchin paused. He put out his woefully thin hand. "Can I join now?"

I fumbled in my pocket. "Yes," I said. I pulled out the coin and pressed it into his palm, which quickly closed into a tight fist. "You have shown a remarkable aptitude for the Young Spies Training League, Boston Company."

There was a communal inhalation of breaths behind the door.

"Now I will give you your first assignment. Are you agreed?"

The lad nodded. "When will I get paid for it?" His voice was almost eager.

"In three days or perhaps even sooner," I said. "If you hear a loud cry in the night, you are to wake your mother, make a great deal of noise, light candles, and call out for the neighbors. That will do. We want to frighten away any bad man who tries to sneak into Bella Edward's house. Do you accept?"

"I accept." The boy thrust his fist beneath his tattered smock.

"Then you are now a member of the Young Spies Training League, Boston Company. Spies never use their own names, you know, so I shall just call you Ferret. I'll come soon for your report, Ferret." With these words I threw a handful of pennies into the void behind the door.

As pandemonium broke out, the Master Spy disappeared.

Chapter Seven

I could hardly contain my eagerness when I returned to Bella Edward's house. At last we had some positive suspects; easy enough to trace the men by their horses. Horses had to be fed, stabled and shod. There were men in Boston who knew every horse in town; its bloodlines, its characteristics, its flaws (above all its flaws), and its owner. These men may not notice the wife's new gown but they could tell you how Mr. Gullible was outwitted by Mr. Sharpie for a spavined chestnut to the tune of six pounds on March eleventh back in 1679.

I had seen the pair of big grays around town. A Huguenot merchant owned the pair; I did not know the man personally but he had close connections to the former Royal Governor, the one we deposed and sent to London in chains for his corrupt regime.

I ran around to the back and pressed a penny into the hand of a startled Abel Keyne. "Your mother gives her permission. This is your first day's pay."

I hurried to the front door, rushed inside and pulled Creasy to his feet. To Esther Thripenny I apologized for my rush, said that Abel would stay the night and that the neighbors would be on the watch for unexpected visitors. Then I dragged Creasy out the door. As soon as we were upon the path, I spoke, keeping my voice low so that we might not be overheard.

"We have names, Creasy! Well, not exactly names. We have a list of horses that came to visit Bella Edwards on a regular basis. The horses didn't come to see Bella, of course, but the owners did." I corrected myself before he could. I went on to tell him about my luck in recruiting an observant young neighbor lad, although I left out the part about the Young Spies Training League, Boston Company. Some people don't understand about fables.

"Yes, that's good," Creasy said. "It will be a simple matter to identify the owners...if they reside in Boston."

"They were observed on a regular basis, which suggests that they came from town." I began to argue but my companion ignored me.

"We found something, too. Mrs. Thripenny didn't realize its significance until I drew it to her attention. We found the cashbox under the bed. It was untouched." Creasy's brows drew into a thin black triangle of puzzlement.

"So?" I prompted the man.

"The cash box, untouched, under the bed. Hetty, the cash box is full of pound notes and gold coins. Why didn't the thief take it? I don't understand. There must be hundreds of pounds in it!"

"Perhaps the thief didn't see it." I shrugged. Why quibble? How fortunate that the box wasn't taken.

"It's not like it was hidden away, Hetty. It's right under the bed. He looked under the pillow...he looked under the bed. We know that because of the fold in the bed hangings. He must have seen the cash box. Why didn't he take it? I don't understand."

Neither did I understand, come to think on it. If you're going to steal an accounts book, why not take the cash? I certainly would have. If I were going to break into someone's house and steal anything, that is, which I certainly had no intentions of doing. I made a hasty apology to my Maker.

Creasy shook his head. "I can only conclude that the thief must be a wealthy man. He does not need the money."

I did not agree with Creasy's conclusion. Who does not need more money? Above others, a wealthy person knows its value. I kept that thought to myself and suggested the obvious.

"Perhaps he heard a noise and thought he would be discovered. He rushed off in a panic."

"Perhaps..." Creasy did not sound convinced. "The thief looked under the pillow. Doesn't this suggest that he was looking for something small in size? What do you keep under your pillow, Hetty?"

"What I keep under my pillow is of no consequence," I said, thinking of a soft leather pouch with a lock of coal black hair inside. "I certainly don't keep my accounts there," I added.

"It was a rhetorical question, Hetty. I mean, what would a woman like Arabella Edwards keep under her pillow? What was the thief seeking there?"

"A love-letter? A locket?" I guessed. "A pair of pearl earrings?" I thought for a moment. "A key?" My voice rose to a squeak.

"Perhaps it's the key to her murder," Creasy said. He lengthened his stride. I quickened my steps to keep up with him.

We passed by Ferret's shack, which was dark and ominous in its silence. I felt twenty beady eyes peering at me from its dark depth. I suppressed a shiver.

"Where does a woman keep her diary?"

Creasy's question came as a welcome diversion. "In the desk where she writes in it. At least that's where I would."

"Might she keep the key under her pillow if there were passages in her diary that she would rather no one saw?"

"Like a nosy old companion, you mean?" I could imagine Esther Thripenny snooping through the pages. I went on. "It would seem more practical to lock up the desk. I assume this was not the case...you found the desk unlocked."

"The desk was kept unlocked," Creasy said.

"Which suggests that whatever she had to hide, Arabella Edwards did not hide it in her desk. Did you look for hidden cubbies?" My desk had a hidden compartment that I used for important papers. Many desks contained these secret depositories.

Creasy rolled his eyes and twisted his lips. "Of course I did. With Mrs. Thripenny's permission, I searched the desk within and without. There were a few bills from tradesmen—for cloth and laces, for provisions—that sort of thing. She had letters from a sister in Portsmouth...in England."

I grabbed his coat sleeve, slowing his stride. "Did you find letters from Edward Ruckenmaul?" I held my breath for his answer.

"No." Creasy shook his head.

"Then she has them hidden away. Depend upon it, Creasy, she has another hiding place." We were halfway down the hill, tidy rows of houses ahead. The waters of the river sparked silver in the distance.

"Bella Edwards was Ruckenmaul's whore for the four years he served as Secretary of the Provinces. She would keep his letters. There may well be secrets in them. Secrets that many of our merchants would rather keep hidden. Who paid the bribes Ruckenmaul demanded? What contracts were received for what payment? Who reviled him in public and did business with the man in private? Oh, there were Boston merchants who acted the hypocrite, I assure you." As a woman in commerce I'd discovered that sharp-practiced businessmen would often confide in me when they should have known better.

"I thought we got rid of Ruckenmaul." Creasy sighed; his shoulders drooped. "When we sent him back to London in chains I thought we were rid of the man."

I understood his despair. Edward Ruckenmaul brought graft and corruption with him to New England. Ship owners had to pay his bribes to unload their ships. His excise men stole our goods and brawled with our citizens. Property owners had to pay anew for land they'd owned for sixty years.

"Maybe Ruckenmaul sent one of his henchmen to collect his letters. Perhaps there is more evidence of his wrongdoing in those letters that would convict him of the charges we brought against him. Perhaps Bella would not surrender the letters and was killed for it!" I could believe any crime of that man.

49

Creasy grabbed my arm, slowing me to a halt. "I don't think so, Hetty. I don't like the man any more than you do, but Esther Thripenny says he was quite generous to Arabella Edwards. He made provisions for her before he left Boston."

"But—" I sputtered in frustration.

"We must look closer to home for the killer, Hetty." Creasy said this in a grave voice. He released my arm.

I fumed in silence, thinking of the injustices the good citizens of Boston suffered under the fist of Secretary Ruckenmaul and of the Tyrant, Royal Governor Edmund Andros.

At the bottom of the hill Creasy's words diverted me.

"That sister in Portsmouth—it seems she took in Arabella's child, a girl of nine years. Arabella sent sums of money for the girl's care."

"Poor child!" I said. "To lose a mother, even a mother as far away as hers. It will not be easy for the child. You shall write to the sister and impart the bad news, Creasy. You will know what to write. It's your duty," I said. If anyone knew his duty, it was Increase Cotton.

Creasy cleared his throat. He slowed his walk.

"What?" I demanded.

"It seems that Arabella sent for the child. In her correspondence of several months ago, Arabella directed the sister to place the child on a ship bound for Boston."

I stopped short. "But...but...that means she will arrive any day now."

Creasy nodded.

My bowels began to churn. Poor child, to come so far and to discover the awful truth of her mother's murder!

"Who will care for her? Who will take her in?" I asked.

"Esther Thripenny will take her, of course. Once I read the letter to her...Arabella only told her a special cargo was coming. It was a complete surprise to the poor old woman, I assure you, Hetty. But she agreed at once to staying on as the child's companion. After all, the house and all that cash will be the child's inheritance."

Goosebumps rose upon my arms, whether at the thought of the old woman as the child's companion or at the thought of the heartbreak that faced the child. And there might be danger to staying in that house.

"Creasy," I said, "we must find out who killed Arabella Edwards, and we must do so without delay!"

Chapter Eight

Our first stop in town was at the smithy, next door to the stables where many of the merchants kept their beasts. I was a good customer of the smith. My mounts were docile, well tended and dependable, with smooth gaits that would carry me for many miles in comfort. It's what I demanded of a horse, since I rode back and forth between Boston and my farm in Rumney Marsh.

The smith put a name to each animal as I described them from the Ferret's observations. The owner of the neat brown mare—an equally neat brown man—was named Oliver Hacker, so the smith informed me.

"I know him," Creasy whispered into my ear. "Hacker was clerk to Secretary Ruckenmaul."

That is interesting, thought I. So the clerk had taken up with the master's mistress? While the cat's away, as they say. Edward Ruckenmaul was one big fat puss that would prey no longer on New England's mice. Collared and belled by the very citizens he'd cheated, taxed and jailed.

The grays were owned by a French Protestant merchant named Gabriel Germaine. Monsieur Germaine had been forced to flee La Rochelle with only the clothes upon his back. Creasy knew the story; what he didn't know was that Germaine fled with a fortune in gold and jewels sewn into the linings. Gabriel Germaine is one of the richest men in Boston.

The owner of the showy black was Harry Kegleigh. I knew

him by sight and by reputation; a loud, boorish fellow who took delight in jeering at the Mathers, father and son. He had the neck of a bull, with square heavy shoulders upon it. His hands were the size of hams.

I could picture him strangling tiny Bella Edwards with no effort at all.

The owner of the chestnut, I did not know. His name was Philip Boynton.

"I'll ask around about him," I murmured to my companion, who nodded.

We left the smithy, walking past the stables where the smell of hay and manure wafted into the street. Creasy suggested we meet again in three hours since he wanted to work on his Lord's Day sermon.

"As my text I'm using *Isaiah: He will swallow up death in victory; and the Lord God will wipe away tears from all faces.*" Creasy swiped at his eyes with a coat sleeve. "Poor child!"

"We'll uncover her mother's murderer," I said, comforting him. "That will be a kind of victory for her—and we've done a good morning's work. We've a list of suspects; we've someone watching the house...I call that a good start." In contrast to his sad countenance, my spirits rose.

"I'll just go order those funeral cakes for Mistress Thripenny," I said, taking my leave. I smiled and gave him a wave of encouragement.

The bake shop was a short distance away on Pudding Lane. I walked with brisk steps, my spirits buoyed by our successes. Creasy had done the impossible; he received permission from Esther Thripenny to search the desk of Arabella Edwards. That he hadn't found anything there was telling in itself. Look for another hiding place. The thief had done just that, it seemed. He'd gone into the kitchen, leaving a full cash box under the bed. What was the significance of the cash box? It worried Creasy but I thought it was fortunate the moneys weren't taken.

The more I considered it, the more I thought the thief had

been frightened away. Perhaps Esther Thripenny had called out in her sleep. Perhaps a floor board creaked, as floor boards do. Perhaps a branch tapped against a window pane. What did it really matter?

The puzzle of the cash box—indeed, the puzzle of the murder—would serve to take Creasy's mind off his late fiancée. I did feel guilt for my former harsh words concerning her, but the truth was often harsh. Creasy had a streak of melancholy that would have been augmented by the deep melancholy of his intended wife. A few years of marriage and the man would be down in the dust, weeping and wailing like his cousin Mather. Perhaps I should tell him! The possibility of turning into another Cotton Mather would frighten him into being as happy as a cat in a creamery. At the thought my smile caused a gentleman to bow to me.

I stifled a giggle as I stepped into Mrs. Dodge's bake shop. Were I blind I would have known it by the Spice Islands scent of ginger and cinnamon that drew me like a pirate to a Spanish galleon. (My first husband, Jack, had captured such a prize. Not that my Jack was a pirate, but an honest privateer.) I jumped as the door banged shut behind me.

Mrs. Dodge looked up at the noise. She stood behind a wide counter where she transferred loaves of crusty bread from a tray into a large woven basket. Mrs. Dodge was noted for her fine white loaves, made from wheat flour that I myself provided to her. The best wheat was raised in the fertile soils of the Albany colony by the industrious Dutch who settled there. I had many good friends among them, for I insisted upon making the trip to inspect the grains for myself.

The baker-lady nodded to me. She reached beneath the counter for a piece of parchment which she twisted into a cone; this cone she filled with a handful of sugared almonds from a large glass jar. The cone she handed to me.

I accepted the gift with thanks, popped one into my mouth and sucked upon the nut as I spoke to her.

"I have come for some funeral cakes for Mrs. Esther Thripenny...the lady that lives on the Tri-mountain." I lisped, gesturing with a crooked finger in the general direction from which I'd come.

"Yes, the order is ready," Mrs. Dodge said her expression properly sober. She reached once more beneath the counter and drew forth a cloth-covered basket.

"Mrs. Dodge, you constantly amaze me," said I. "This is service indeed!" I'd barely time to give the order and there it was, waiting for me. Well, a good merchant anticipates his customer's need, as my late second husband, Mr. Henry, used to say.

Before I could further compliment the lady the door banged behind me. I turned with an involuntary start. The man in the tea-colored cloak stood just inside the door.

"You!" I cried out.

The man dared stare at me as if I were unknown to him. He stepped across the floor to the counter, turning an indifferent gaze from me to the shop owner. Although he stood only an arm's length from me, he ignored me completely.

"Why have you followed me here?" I demanded of the man.

"I beg your pardon?" The man pretended to be startled.

I took a step towards him, shaking a finger close to his face. Ignore me at his peril. "Why have you followed me here?"

The man in the tea cloak stepped back. He raised his palms to me, as if to protect himself. "I assure you, madam, I have not followed you here. You are unknown to me."

"Mrs. Henry..." The shop owner looked from me to the gentleman.

"You followed me down from the Tri-mountain yesterday." My finger pointed at his nose. I saw the flash of recognition in his eyes; he could not deny my charge.

"I did not follow you anywhere, madam."

The rogue! The varlet! The bold-faced liar! I shook my finger at him. "You followed me down from Arabella Edwards's house. I saw you." I could not keep the triumph from my voice.

The man lowered his palms slowly. "I walked down from the Tri-mountain yesterday, yes, but I was not following you, madam."

"Why did you hide behind a tree, then, when I looked back?" I lowered my finger but I took another step towards him. I had him backed against the counter.

"Mrs. Henry..." Mrs. Dodge attempted to speak.

Neither of us noticed her. The man in the tea cloak straightened with an effort. He drew the cloak about him. "If you must know, madam, I had to piss."

"Oh," I said, stepping back. The man was clever, very clever. His eyes were nearly the color of his cloak.

"Then why did you follow me to the chandler shop on Fish Street? Why did you wait for me outside? You were spying on me," I accused the man, my voice rising.

"Wait outside the—?" The man's own voice faltered. "I don't know what you mean, madam. I had an errand on Fish Street, not that that's any of your business." The tea eyes narrowed.

"Oh, so you would have it all coincidence," I scoffed.

"You just happened to come from Edwards' house, you just happened to go to Fish Street and you just happened to come into Mrs. Dodge's bake shop this morning." I stressed the word *happened*. The man tugged at his cloak. Caught out in his lies, the fool was nervous, I could see. But the rogue confounded me in his oily voice.

"Madam, I have come here to pick up some funeral cakes which I ordered yesterday evening. The cakes are for my mother, who lives upon the Tri-mountain."

The slick rogue! The knave!

Mrs. Dodge confirmed the man's answer, saying that he had indeed ordered cakes for Mistress Esther Thripenny.

"Mistress Thripenny said nothing to me of a son, sir," I continued to argue. "And your name is Phinny, Sir, not Thripenny."

The man glared at me with the tea eyes of a tiger. "That, madam, is a personal matter between me and my mother. All I will say is that I chose to shorten my name to Phinny. In my childhood I was called Ephrata Thripenny."

I nearly dropped my cone of sugared almonds.

The man turned a frosty shoulder to me and addressed Mrs. Dodge with his full attention.

"You have the cakes ready for me?"

I slunk across the floor and opened the shop door, taking care that it made no noise as I released it. I did not care to draw attention to my beet-red face.

Chapter Nine

"You haven't spoken much, Hetty. Here I've been spouting off to you about my sermon and you're silent as a clam. Do you disagree with my text? Am I stressing the wrong points?" Creasy leaned over the table as he spoke, peering into my eyes.

We sat over dinner at Milk's Tavern. I picked at my fish pie. "No, no...you are very generous towards a woman that many would scorn as a whore. It's not your text. I like your sermon very well."

"Then what? Are you worried about our forthcoming interviews?" His eyes remained upon mine, soft with concern like a dog at the feet of its master. "It's not pleasant to think that the gentleman to whom you're speaking may be a murderer, but you'll be safe, I promise."

I shook my head. "I'm not frightened, Creasy. There's not much the murderer can do to us in the light of day with so many people about. Besides, we do have the weight of the magistrates behind us. We have a right to question them. It's either speak to us or speak to the walls of a jail cell. At least we are spared one interview." I proceeded to tell him of my meeting in the bake shop.

"I still think he followed me yesterday," I added.

"A son?" Creasy fell back into his seat. "Esther Thripenny has a son? But she made no mention of a son. I understood that she had no family, didn't you? What is the woman about?

I shall have to speak to her...perhaps later today, if I have time." The thin black brows drew into a knot.

I set aside my plate and reached for the mug of cider. The tangy liquid soothed my dry throat. If my humiliation at the bake-shop rankled, I had better put my feelings aside. Best to concentrate upon our task. We must discover where the different gentlemen were at the time of Bella Edward's murder. I set down the empty mug with a clank and wiped my mouth with my sleeve.

Creasy rose. I sighed and stood up.

Our first gentleman, the Ferret's neat brown man on the neat brown mare, was Oliver Hacker, former clerk to the former Secretary of the Provinces, the detested Edward Ruckenmaul. Hacker greeted us with cold composure, submitting to our questioning in the same manner. The man sat upon a plain high wooden stool before a high clerk's desk in his plain brown office of wood and leather. A small wooden chair was the only other piece of furniture, which seat Creasy surrendered to me. Before us were shelves of neatly stacked ledgers. I found it difficult to imagine the man in the throes of passion, even with such a temptress as Arabella Edwards.

With movements of calm deliberation, Mister Hacker produced a diary bound in leather, flicked it open to the date of June 10, and turned it so that we could see the entry for that date. He had been employed all day in tallying the cargo of the ship, the Black Rose at Bull's Wharf off Flounder Lane.

Tallying cargo is a precise, time-consuming and public task, so I eliminated Mister Hacker as a suspect in the murder providing, of course, that his alibi held. I would have a clerk from my own wharf run over to Bull's and confirm it. I nodded at Creasy to continue his questioning.

His Tuesday visits to Arabella Edwards were of a business nature and private, he insisted. "I am not at liberty to discuss it. I remain her agent in commerce and shall act in the lady's best interests until such time as I am relieved of my duties." Hacker's thin lips tightened.

He could not be moved from that stance, even though Creasy pointed out that the lady was deceased.

"Murdered, sir...most foully and brutally murdered. Do you not wish to see her murderer captured? Do you not wish to see justice done for the poor woman?" Creasy raised his voice to a shout.

Answering that he could not help us, Hacker politely and firmly showed us to the door.

Our reception by Harry Kegleigh began with a hearty greeting from that thick-set gentleman.

"Come in, come in, good sir and fair lady. How may I help you? A Bible box for the gentleman? I've a new arrived shipment of cloths for the lady...a lustering of pale yellow would make up into a fine gown for this lovely woman..."

Kegleigh looked me up and down. He'd chosen the right color to interest me but that was not why we'd come, more's the pity. I gazed around the room at shelves full of bundles and boxes.

Creasy drew himself up to his full height. He was taller than the gentleman before us but about half the gentleman's girth. "Sir, my name is Increase Cotton, minister to the Summer Street Church. We have come to ask you some questions about the late Arabella Edwards. Is there some place where we can be private?"

Kegleigh's jovial manner changed at Creasy's words. Thick eyebrows drew into a frown, his voice was curt. "This way, sir." He led us through the shop to the back of the building. We passed through another room where men in leather aprons carried boxes and bundles from one place to another while others stood bent over boxes, sorting goods.

We were shown into a small room, as cluttered an office as Oliver Hacker's was plain and neat. There was barely room to stand, much less to sit, so we stood inside the doorway.

"Mister Increase Cotton, is it?" Kegleigh placed big fists upon his hips and looked Creasy over. "Ah yes...one of the mewling Mathers. I've heard of ye, young milk-sop."

I interceded before my companion could respond, holding out my hand. "I am Mehitable Henry, sir." I introduced myself in my sweetest voice. "I am a cousin by marriage to Mister Cotton here, and his assistant in determining what happened to the poor woman lately deceased." I smiled prettily and fluttered my eyelashes at the man. I have often found this a means of diffusing tension. It worked.

Kegleigh swallowed both my hands within his huge mitts. Of necessity we stood close yet he managed to bend and kiss each wrist in turn.

"My great pleasure, Mrs. Henry," he purred. "I have long sought an introduction to the lovely Mehitable Henry. It's been difficult for my hard head to grasp that such a pretty little thing could be a successful merchant in trade, yet I know ye are such." He kept my hands prisoner within his own while he inspected me...but not the way he had inspected Creasy.

I managed to slide back my right foot and make a slight curtsy to acknowledge his compliment. Next to me I caught Creasy's expression of distaste.

"Sir," I spoke with haste, "we have come to you for help."

"Aye, Madam, command me. I am your servant." He murmured to me, his green eyes glinting.

He looked as hungry as a wolf in winter.

I began once more. "We have come on behalf of Mistress Arabella Edwards, lately deceased. I'm sure you've heard of her death." I gazed up into the wolf eyes, keeping my own as round and guileless as a sylvan pool.

"Aye, I've heard. Poor lass. Poor lass." Kegleigh rubbed my hands softly within his great paws.

I wasn't sure whether he meant Arabella or me. I rather thought I'd be the poor lass if I fell into his clutches. Fortunate for me that I was immune to his charms. For Harry Kegleigh exuded a rough and powerful kind of attraction. I went on to address him lest my companion spoil the mood.

"There is no one to speak for her. That is why we have come on Mistress Edward's behalf. Would you tell me about her, sir?" I raised my eyes in innocent appeal, ignoring the greedy gleam within Kegleigh's.

"Oh, Bella was a real beauty, and she'd a good head on her shoulders with it. Good company, she was...could drink with a fellow and laugh with a fellow and...other things."

He leered down at me with this yet I thought he spoke of Bella Edwards with sincerity. I felt free to ask him: "Why would anyone want to harm her?"

Kegleigh raised one eyebrow thick as a caterpillar. "Who knows? Jealousy, perhaps. We men are jealous brutes." The caterpillar brow waggled at me.

I giggled involuntarily at the sight.

"Enchanting, madam," Kegleigh murmured. "I can see you've driven a few fellows mad with your own sweet face."

I lowered my lashes in modesty while Creasy grunted next to me. But he had sense enough not to interfere.

"Yes...yes...you've the power in you to drive a man mad. That mouth, those eyes...oh, a man could drown himself in those emerald eyes of yours."

The voice caressed me in a throaty, hypnotic growl.

The spell was broken by the abrupt demand of Creasy Cotton. "What was your relationship to Arabella Edwards?"

Kegleigh's eyes left mine for a quick glance at my companion. "Why minister, what do ye think a man does with a pretty woman?" He smiled down at me. "Here, I'll show ye."

My captured hands were thrust behind me into the small of my back, forcing me against Kegleigh. My nether region pressed into his while his mouth covered mine, his lips hard and wet as if he would suck out my soul. I could not back away, so I stood rigid and unresponsive. Then I slid my right foot back and kicked him as hard as I could in the shin.

Kegleigh released me. It was he who fell back, cursing and hopping on one foot. There was a black smudge upon the white stocking; I noted this with satisfaction.

I grabbed Creasy's arm, preventing him from striking Kegleigh with his balled fists. "Come, Creasy...we'll get no more from this boorish fellow." I dragged him bodily out the door, ignoring his resistance and pulling him through the storeroom.

"The rogue...the villain!" Creasy sputtered. "How dare he insult you? This isn't over. I'll teach the brute some manners. Milk-sop, am I? I'll show him who's a milk-sop, the great. oaf. I'm not afraid of him."

Creasy would have pulled away but I kept a firm grip upon his arm. I steered him down the street, away from possible disaster. "Pay him no mind, Creasy. Don't let him distract you from our mission, which is to discover the killer of Arabella Edwards. We'll find a way to discover Kegleigh's whereabouts on the night Bella was murdered. (So I thought of the woman, such an intimate picture I had built in my mind of her.)

I kept up a flow of chatter to distract the man. "He is an oaf indeed," I said, agreeing with my companion in a calm voice. "He is a fool, and beneath your notice, Creasy. Kegleigh is no gentleman and he doesn't know how to kiss a woman, either." I rubbed my mouth with my free hand.

Creasy's face brightened. "He doesn't?"

"He does not." I was firm. "You are much better at it than he is, and I do not mean to flatter you. It's the truth." I shrugged.

"I am? I mean...the fellow deserves a whipping for his unmannerly behavior."

I noted with relief that Creasy's tone held more censure than anger in it.

"Well, I unmanned him, I think. There are times when a kick in the shins is more effective than a whipping." I felt a sense of satisfaction recalling the solid thud of my shoe against the bone of his ankle. "Bested by a mere female—a brute like that feels it worse than the whip."

Creasy stopped short, bringing me to a halt beside him since I still held his coat sleeve.

"Perhaps that's what happened to Arabella Edwards. Perhaps she got the better of Kegleigh. If that's the case, you must take care, Hetty. Keep your distance from that man." His voice was stern and urgent.

He was concerned for my safety, well so was I at the thought. Had Harry Kegleigh's ham-sized hands strangled the breath out of Arabella Edwards? Had he further humiliated the woman by hanging her next to a condemned witch? Would a kick in the shins be cause for similar treatment? My thoughts must have shown in my face for Creasy turned me around bodily and pointed me in the direction of my rooms.

"I'm taking you home."

I let him.

Chapter Ten

It's not that I was frightened, but I felt frustrated and exhausted by two encounters with men where I was insulted or made to look like a fool. After Creasy saw me safely to my rooms above the warehouse, I went straight to my bed and to sleep.

My favorite brood sow Priscilla came ambling towards me carrying a woven basket in her pink snout. Priscilla set the basket at my feet and I bent to remove the napkin that covered the basket's contents. There upon a velvet cushion lay a lovely fashion baby displaying an exquisite daffodil gown. The fashion baby had long, flowing locks of gold and painted eyes of a brilliant blue in an ivory-carved face. I had never seen such beautiful work.

I reached over the basket to pick up the fashion baby when it sat up and laughed. I drew my hand back as if I had been burned. The thing lifted her skirts and climbed out of the basket. With incredible speed for such tiny legs it ran round and round the basket. I tried to grasp it but it eluded my fingers and went running across the room. Priscilla went after it with a disapproving grunt. I yelled at the pig to stop, fearing its great bulk would smash the little creature to pieces.

Priscilla ignored my commands, gaining upon the fashion baby with four fast legs. The tiny thing skittered around a chair with Priscilla hard upon her. The pig slammed into the chair, sending it across the floor with one leg broken off and jagged splinters of wood flying in every direction. The pig's pink snout hugged the floor, sniffing out its prey in the confusion of wood chips. The fashion baby dived for a knothole in the pine floorboard; it turned into a yellow snake and slithered down the hole to escape.

Priscilla squealed in rage, stomping upon the hole with her sharp trotters. Tiny peals of laughter echoed up from the knothole until it filled the room in ghostly mockery. I pressed my hands over my ears to dim the sounds.

My own groan woke me. I opened my eyes expecting to find Priscilla next to the bed. Forcing my groggy mind to focus, I reasoned that Priscilla was safe in Rumney Marsh where she belonged. No doubt the pig was grubbing in the green shoots of the marshes or slobbering up wild strawberries in the fields. I'd been dreaming, that's all.

I pulled myself up from the bed and staggered over to the wash basin. Ignoring the cloth, I caught up cool pools of water in my hands and splashed droplets over my face. Light from my window told me it was late afternoon. I'd slept the day away and felt the worse for it, my groggy head pounding until I realized there was someone at the door. I managed to tuck back loose strands of hair and to straighten my gown as I stumbled through the sitting room to answer the summons. (I had only the two rooms plus kitchen in the back; it was good enough for my first marriage and it was good enough for me now.)

"Hetty...are you there?" A well known voice called out.

"Just a minute," I grumbled, fumbling to lift the bar. I pulled open the door.

"Hetty..." Creasy stood there with brows lifted in surprise. "Are you well?"

That I must look a sight did nothing to ease my temper. "Of course, I'm well. I'm always well. I was just napping, that's all. Come in." I motioned none too gracefully and Creasy stepped inside, taking care to avoid my person.

"You'll have to give me a moment to put myself together," I said, fuming at his lack of gallantry. But then, Creasy was often blunt. He spoke without thinking; a trait that cost him where women were concerned.

66

"I banked the fire this morning before I left. Would you start it again for me...please?" I added the latter to show the man that one does not neglect one's manners, even if one shows some neglect in appearance.

In my chamber I caught up the looking glass and shuddered at what I saw reflected there. Red, puffy eyes; hair hanging down in strands; one cheek creased with pillow lines; not to mention the crushed skirts of my gown. I've got to find a personal servant, I thought for the hundredth time. Good help was difficult to keep, especially in Boston. I'd had the perfect servant, efficient and willing to work, but I'd given her her freedom papers—Zillah was brought in a slave from the West Indies. I missed her but I did not regret granting her freedom. No one can own another human being. I could advertise for a slave or an indentured servant but the same thing would probably happen. I grabbed the brush and pulled it through my hair.

Having made myself somewhat more presentable—a clean apron, hair tied by a pink ribbon—I joined Creasy in the kitchen. I found him kneeling by the hearth where be nursed a small flame beneath a fresh stack of kindling. The flame caught and soon reproduced into a cheery blaze of reds, blues, oranges and golds. I went about the room lighting the wall sconces then I hung the kettle over the hearth.

"Let's have some India tea," I suggested, being partial to the new beverage. Cousin Cotton Mather had informed me of its healthful and medicinal properties.

Creasy nodded. He took a seat at the small gateleg table I used for my usually solitary dining while I rummaged through the cupboard for my box of tea leaves, a steeping pot and two wooden toddy cups. I set out small bowls of nuts and raisins. Soon the exotic fragrance of far-away lands filled my nostrils as I poured out two cups of the steaming infusion.

We sat in companionable silence, sipping and nibbling, like an old married couple. Except that I had vowed never to marry again. And my affections were not for the man across the table.

Nor were they for that big brute Harry Kegleigh. At the thought of that man my nose wrinkled in disapproval.

"I'm sorry I left you on your own today, Creasy," I apologized. "I hope you don't think me a coward. It's just that I felt so frustrated—first that run-in at the bake-shop, then to be kissed by that vulgar fellow—I felt the need for some quiet. I made a mistake in taking a nap...I had such a strange dream! What I should have done was to go straight to the office and to work on my accounts. That's what I should have done. How did you get on?"

Creasy looked up from his cup of steaming brew. "Very well. That's what I came to tell you." He grinned, his eyes narrowing and barely concealing a twinkle.

"We are invited to a grand dinner to be held on Friday next. What do you think of that?"

I could tell that he was very pleased with himself. "To whom do we owe the honor of this invitation?" I asked.

"To Monsieur Gabriel Germaine, the Huguenot merchant. He will invite those people who were supporters of the former Royal Governor—those who were acquaintances of Arabella Edwards. And you need not worry about Harry Kegleigh—he shan't be invited. M'sieur Germaine says Kegleigh was not one of that crew. M'sieur Germaine thinks Kegleigh is a great villain and more than likely the one who killed Mistress Edwards."

I was inclined to agree with this assessment. "You have done very well, Creasy. And how did this come about?" I asked. "What did you do after you left me here? Come, tell me all! Wait...I'll pour some more India tea for us."

This done, I seated myself, eager to hear Creasy's tale. He had certainly wasted no time while I lay a slug-a-bed.

Creasy took a sip from his wooden cup, cleared his throat and began. "Well, I was on my way home when I saw that pair of grays and the carriage stopped in the street. The gentleman leaned out the carriage window to speak to a man. I didn't hesitate, Hetty, I just walked up to the carriage, introduced myself and asked for a word."

Creasy looked at me with raised brows, as if amazed at his own daring. I nodded to encourage him.

"M'sieur Germaine was most cordial, Hetty. He suggested that he drive me home, that we could speak in private on the way. You should have seen my neighbors when I drove up in that carriage! Old Mistress Pitkin nearly fell out the window gawking."

This caused me to smirk; I could almost wish the old gossip had fallen out on her head. On many occasions I'd been the butt of her jibes, uttered in a voice loud enough for the street to hear: "Bold Jezebel...haughty jangling daughter of Zion..." Those were a few of her comments on my visits to see Creasy, who is minister to the church on Summer Street and a colleague in the investigation of several awful crimes.

We are both cousins of Cotton Mather and his wife, Abigail. Cousin Mather has a tendency to fall into bouts of melancholia when he is consulted about crimes of a delicate nature, which are beyond the scope of the local constable. Instability of any kind frays his sensitive nerves. Creasy has gotten into the habit of filling in for his more renowned relative, feeling his knowledge of guilt in the human soul gives him an insight into solving these crimes. I feel it my duty to carry on my late second husband's mission as a magistrate to restore the safety of the community. Mr. Henry would approve, although Cousin Mather does not like my interference. Creasy, I think, has grown used to it. Besides, I have connections to both high and low societies that is of benefit when information is needed, and the wealth to pay for it. Yes, between us, Creasy and I make a formidable team.

"M'sieur Germaine was very open with me upon the drive," Creasy went on. I told him we were looking into the death of Mistress Arabella Edwards and he wished us success in our search. He admitted to being enamored of the woman, even when she was...ah...Secretary Ruckenmaul's whore. When we sent Ruckenmaul back to London in chains, M'sieur proposed that Mistress Edwards become his mistress. He told her that he would take care of her...that she need not fear her reduced circumstances."

"And what did Bella Edwards say to that?" I asked. I thought this proposal rather pompous, myself, but I suppose if one were desperate a woman would welcome having her future secured.

"M'sieur said that she only laughed and said he need not worry for her circumstances; that Edward Ruckenmaul had seen to it that she was well provided. She said that M'sieur was welcome to visit her once a week, that she had always liked him." Creasy's face flushed; he went on in rapid words. "This is what he told me, Hetty. M'sieur Germaine was very frank, but I assure you it was not in a boasting manner at all. He spoke to me...well, as one man to another."

One man to another? I nearly sniggered. It was obvious that Creasy was impressed with the Huguenot merchant; he made a point of pronouncing the gentleman's name with a French accent. I could not resist a little poke at that bit of vanity with a poor pronunciation of my own. "And *Monsoor* spoke with such frankness to a minister of the Reformed Church?"

"M'sieur Germaine knew that I would understand his frailty and accept his repentance for his behavior. He is an unmarried gentleman, as he pointed out."

As if that would excuse everything, I thought. "Yes, well that explains the money in the cash box beneath the bed," I said with a shrug.

"Also, we shall meet Phillip Boynton at this dinner. Perhaps you can find out more about the man before then."

Creasy looked at me as if he expected my praise. I wasn't quite ready to oblige.

"Did you ask *Monsoor* where he was on the night Arabella Edwards was murdered?"

Creasy set down his cup. "Of course I did, Hetty, and he was out on the West Frontier—near old Mister Eliot's Praying Indian Towns. The Huguenot refugees would like to found their own plantation there. Isn't that admirable?"

"He went with a company of fellow refugees?" I asked. It

would be impossible for *Monsoor* to travel to the West Frontier and to be in Salem upon the same day.

"He went with one of the Praying Indians as guide, he said. M'sieur Germaine was to look about for land on their behalf."

"Oh." I must have sounded skeptical.

"The Praying Indians are as trustworthy Christians as you or I," Creasy said in objection to my tone.

"I didn't say anything."

"You were thinking it." Creasy accused me with a frown. "You think he has no way to account for his whereabouts just because he was in the company of an Indian."

I forbore to mention the historical fact that in the late war against King Phillip much of the devastation was caused by Praying Indians who deserted their Christian beliefs and joined their pagan brothers. Nor did I care to remind him of a certain Mohawk leader in the Albany colony whom we both knew. I did think of Blue Bear when I spoke, however. "When a native man gives his word it is a point of honor with him, I know that much," I said. "If you can find this Praying Indian and he says that he took the Huguenot out to the Praying Indian towns that day, I shall accept his word."

I wasn't in the mood to argue with the man. Creasy takes delight in disputation, a form of argument that appears to prove that man can fly if he honks like a goose. I got up and busied myself in assembling a light supper. I set out a platter of meats and cheeses, two pewter plates and two mugs. Into the mugs I poured cool, frothy ale. An effective remedy for a tendency to disputation is to fill the goose's beak with food and drink.

Chapter Eleven

After Creasy's visit, I felt the need for fresh air to clear my head. I left the warehouse and walked out onto the wharf, where I took deep breaths of the wharf-scent: rotting wood and dead fish. Ah, there is nothing like the smell of one's livelihood! Above me the stars sparkled like diamonds; over my head loomed a forest of masts creaking softly with the gentle waves of black water that lapped like hungry kittens at the swelling hulls.

How could I shut myself off from this balmy evening? A short walk, I decided, only a short walk in the company of my fellow man. I'd napped, my energy surged anew and the soft breezes lured me into movement. Turning, the firefly lights of the Town beckoned; window candles blinking, lanterns winking, pine-knot torches flaring the way for coaches and chairs. As a moth to the flame, my steps were directed to Fish Street and to the bridge over Mill Creek that led to the Town Square.

Nor was I alone in my wanderings. A horde of people passed me by, coming and going from the square; laborers, carters, sailors, servants, goodwives with children in tow, merchants on foot and on horseback. Busy in reflections of an affectionate nature, I was unaware of the hordes. Only the swain and his sweetheart caught my attention. They strolled in a leisurely fashion, as did I, their glances only for each other. I smiled. A spirit of good will suffused my being. I did not envy the courting couples. Although the object of my affectionate thoughts was unavailable to me at the moment, I did not feel alone. There are rare times of harmony that infect every person upon the streets; this night was one.

Like a shade I glided across the bridge to the town dock, joining many others who milled about in small groups, chattering or watching the entertainments the evening offered. Lanterns and bonfires sprang up like mushrooms on a rainy day, lighting the square. Here a group of young men rang bells and banged upon drums. Within a circle of cheering men, two stout, red-faced boys wrestled with grunts and strained cries. Peddlers called out their wares of cakes and gingerbreads; old women offered mugs of herbed beer drawn from buckets by their sides. Before the skeletal masts of their sloops, three sailors danced jigs and hornpipes as piped by a black-skinned comrade.

My attention was drawn by a chapman who bawled out the latest confessions of a murderer, but it was only an old execution sermon of Cotton Mather's preaching. Cousin Cotton was a favorite of those in need of an execution sermon; his way with words brought tears of repentance from many a murderous eye. I wandered away from the stall to watch a young apprentice contort himself into various and puzzling shapes, much to the raggings of his peers. It was as if a spontaneous country fair had sprung out of the balmy evening breezes. If I walked around with a foolish grin upon my face, I was one of many.

Even the town crier beamed good will as he recited a poem on "The Scourge of Drunkenness" to a sober-reflecting group of men and women. I paused to listen. The rhyme was poor but the poet wrote from knowledge, I thought. To encourage the poor fellow and to applaud the sentiments, I clapped.

A laborer in a striped smock and knee breeches approached the town crier, spoke briefly to him and handed the crier a sheet of paper. The man, his blond hair tied back with a blue ribbon, stepped back to listen, arms crossed, his legs spread wide.

An ode to his lady-love, no doubt. Curious, I stayed to hear the verses. I could not see the man's face, but the fellow had broad shoulders and he showed a good leg in green wool stockings. I noted that the laborer wore shoes of good quality leather with silver plate buckles.

The town crier's lips moved in silent perusal of the paper he held. He cleared his throat before he began his reading. An ode to a lady-love it proved to be, the town crier emphasizing the poet's ardor with uplifted hand and smiting of chest. I listened with growing impatience to praises of "*golden curls... ruby lips... mirthful laugh... teeth like pearls...*" I turned my back to watch a more artful performance of juggling. The young man kept up six balls in the air. How do they do that? I marveled at his dexterity.

Behind me the Town Crier bellowed out a refrain: "*And all golden is her hair/ as she dances in the air.*"

Then came lines about bells. "*There are bells....*" This was repeated over and over.

'Yes, yes,' I thought, tugging at a curl that hung loose beneath my white cap, "so there are *happy bells, urgent bells, call-to-meeting bells....* Everyone knows that." I suppose the young man's lady-love thinks him a New World Lovelace, if I might insult the cavalier poet. (I wouldn't sully the name of the great Milton by even thinking of them together.)

I turned to see how the proud poet accepted his words but the young prodigy was not to be seen. Perhaps he skulked off in shame.... The Town Crier boomed out the last stanzas:

> *The bell that tolls the grave*
> *Rang ma belle her doom,*
> *Greed for gold did maul her*
> *She lies now in the gloom.*
> *Her golden glow is dimmed now*
> *And hidden in the tomb.*
> *And all golden was her hair*
> *As she danced upon the air.*

The skin prickled upon the back of my neck as the town crier lowered his bewigged head, a beefy hand clasped to his breast in sorrow.

A woman sobbed and the man next to me wiped a tear from his eye with a square of linen. The people who had gathered for the town crier's recitation all applauded. I lurched forward to accost the town crier.

"Who wrote that? Where is he? What is his name? Let me see that." I reached for the paper but the town crier held the verse beyond my reach. He frowned down at me.

"Madam, restrain yourself!" His words boomed out above the crowd. People turned.

I drew back a step and took a deep breath. "Please, sir, this is important to me. Will you tell me the name of the gentleman who wrote these verses?" Glancing down at my hands, I saw that I had clasped them. I pulled them apart. Then I sought in my pocket for a coin.

The town crier had drawn himself up, glaring at me in disapproval. I produced the coin. He peered down at the shiny object I held for his inspection. He cleared his throat, looked at the paper and spoke in a measured tone.

"*Leman Urck*...that is the gentleman's name. The verse is entitled: *The Golden Belle,* spelled with an E."

"Leman Urck? I know of no such family. Who is he?" I twisted the coin between my fingers.

"Never met the young man before in my life." The answer was prompt and certain.

"Where is he? Where did he go? Do you see him?"

We both scanned the crowd. The crier was taller than me by far, but he had no more success than I did in locating the man who called himself *Leman Urck*. Patently a false name, I thought. But the verses were about Arabella Edwards, I was sure of that. The constant reference: "*There are bells....*" What else but a play upon her name? That's what had finally caught my attention, not the "golden hair," or the "ruby lips." Then there was the reference to "*maul,*" as in Edward Ruckenmaul, her former protector. But the words that caused a shiver to run up and down my spine were in the refrain, when I realized that the poor girl *dancing in the air* was a poetic way of describing the gallows dance.

I asked the Crier to give me the paper of verses and held out the coin.

He eyed the object before shaking his head. "I can't let you have it just yet, Madam. The young man paid for the week's reading. I am to read it here in the Square every evening at this time for a week. The young man was most emphatic upon the point."

I could not refrain from a snort of disgust. This might well be the killer within my grasp. Would I have to call in the constable to gather the evidence? I did not want to have to run to Constable Phillymort for anything. He'd only inform the magistrates of my incompetence and remind them that they had chosen me—well, Creasy, actually—over him for this work. Not that the constable wasn't a thorough man, but he lacked imagination. And he bullied people with his authority. Creasy and I, between us, were successful in several instances of solving murders that called for imagination and discretion.

"Well then," I said, "can you at least make a copy of it for me? Have it here tomorrow evening and I'll pay you the worth of two week's readings." I handed him the one coin.

The town crier accepted the coin, pocketing it with a nod of his curling wig.

"Have we a rival here for Mister Urck's affections?" He gave me a broad wink, which was meant as much for the audience around us. "Since one of the ladies is in the tomb, I wager I know the one who'll marry him." He looked around for approval at this jest. Several people laughed.

I clamped shut my mouth lest I tell him what I thought of his poor wit. I needed that copy of the verses. As I marched away, he called out.

"Don't be too hard upon the lad—it's only a pretty verse, even if 'twere meant for another lady."

Another lady? As if I would be jealous of another lady! I didn't even know the young man, but if I did, he would not be writing verse to another lady. The town crier was an oaf.

The crowds of people no longer amused me; the balmy evening seemed less appealing to me than my rooms and quiet from babbling fools. Pen and paper, that's what I needed, and a copy of those verses. Leman Urck... how ridiculous. Leman, I knew, was an old word for lover. Edward Ruckenmaul had been Bella's lover. No doubt there were others, but he was connected to the poem. Why? What had the former Secretary of the Provinces had to do with her murder? Ruckenmaul was in London—we'd sent him there in chains. The man would not dare return to Massachusetts Bay, he was detested by the populace here. (The feeling was returned by him with mutual passion.) Much as I'd like to see the man hanged, it wouldn't be for the murder of his mistress.

I paused at the Mill Creek Bridge and stood looking over the wooden railing. Lights from the bonfires were reflected in the dark waters below as I contemplated this puzzle. Of course! I slapped my head with my hand. Leman Urck.... It was a simple anagram for Ruckenmaul. But the man with the verse was not Edward Ruckenmaul—I wish I knew who he was. And why had he made public that verse? The poem was to be read every night for a week. Why? Did the poet mean to reach someone with that verse?

My tired brain cried out for relief from this confusion. I needed my bed. As I hastened down Fish Street the noise from the Square behind me receded. I was thankful for it. By the docks here it was deserted and blissfully quiet. I slowed my walk, which had been nearly a trot. Past Lakes wharf there was an empty lot where the harbor waters crept up to the land; a brief open space. That's where the attack occurred.

Chapter Twelve

Two hands reached out from the shadows and I was pushed hard against the warehouse wall. Before I could cry out a rag muffled my protest with ruthless efficiency. I was gagged, my hands tied behind me, my gown tied across my knees and a grain bag thrust down over my helpless body. I knew it was a grain bag because the dry chaff filled my nostrils until I thought I would choke. A series of sneezes rescued me from that particular disaster but I wondered what other fate awaited me.

I was swept up by strong arms, carried to the water and dropped into the bottom of a dory like a sack of rye. My head hit the wooden seat. The craft rocked in an alarming motion as it was shoved into the water and my attacker jumped in. I heard the oarlocks creak, then we settled into a steady, quick rhythm. While I couldn't see a thing, I could feel the sway of the boat and hear the gentle lap of the waters. Was I being rowed out to the deep waters where the larger vessels anchored? Would I be smuggled on board and set sail upon the seas, an unwilling passenger to an unknown destination? Or would I be rowed out to the deep and simply dropped overboard, bound and helpless, to drown? He wouldn't dare drop me into the harbor - my body would float into shore and be discovered. I tried to take a deep breath to steady my fears, but I only sneezed.

The dory skimmed across the harbor. I strained to listen for any sound that might tell me where we were headed. In the distance the laughter and cheers of the crowd receded. Oh, how I longed to join them once again, to see the bright fires, to watch the juggler, to marvel as the lad contorted his body into a Gordian knot. Oh, how I longed for the sword of Alexander that I might slice through the Gordian knots that held me captive in this accursed craft! Struggle was useless; I could only move my head, and only to bump it against the seat as I did.

I could feel very little motion as steady, powerful strokes propelled the little craft through the waters. I was a little relieved, because we kept to a course in the harbor. If we were heading for deeper waters, the waves would get rougher, the motion much rockier. No, we were cutting across to the south end of town, I was certain of it. He did not mean to drown me, then. So long as I was in Boston, I could manage any threat.

The trip across the harbor probably took ten minutes, but it seemed an endless voyage. My head ached; my limbs were cramped from my enforced position, which was curled up in the bottom of a dory. No matter what was to come, the scrape of the dory bottom hitting sand brought me relief. Again the little craft rocked as my assailant leaped out and dragged the boat ashore.

I was lifted up like a sack of grain, thrown over a broad shoulder and jounced up and down as he jogged across dry land. I felt dizzy; the bag stifled me. I could not help groaning as he hopped up a set of stairs. I felt every lurch in my bones. I heard the click of a latch, the sound of a door opening, more bouncing, another door, and I was thrown face down onto a soft surface.

The grain bag was torn open. The rope that confined my hands fell away, the rag removed from my mouth. I rolled over, blinking at the bright light of candles and of a crackling fire in the hearth. I could not focus my eyes, but I knew it was Harry Kegleigh who stood over me by his vast bulk. He threw off his cloak and shrugged himself out of a waistcoat, standing there in a white smock like a large, hairy ape. My vision returned in time to see the huge grin that split his face.

"You wanted to know what I did with Bella. Well, this is it. She liked to be abducted. There are women who enjoy being forced, you know. Bella liked me to tie her up. She became a tigress in bed when we played at kidnapping. You are a woman of spirit; I could tell that at once." Kegleigh rolled up one sleeve. "I like women of spirit."

The brute began to spin like a top before my eyes. I struggled to sit up, my mouth wet with saliva. A lump of lead the size of Kegleigh's fist lay heavy in my gut.

"Go ahead and fight me," Harry Kegleigh said. "I hope you will."

I lunged for the side of the bed.

Kegleigh was quick but not quick enough.

I vomited all over the side of the bed and onto the floor, drenching the bed linens in puke.

"I'm sorry," I groaned.

Kegleigh placed a basin under my chin and held it steady while my mouth and nose gushed like a geyser. I could feel the sour taste and smell of rye grains as they dripped from my nose. Then and there I made a silent vow to never eat rye bread again.

I give credit to Kegleigh, who murmured encouraging things to me: "That's right, get it all out. You'll feel better."

I could not help but oblige. Finally, after a bout of dry heaves, I had nothing left to contribute and fell back upon the bed.

"Strangle me now, Kegleigh, with your bare hands. Death shall come as a release." Such were my thoughts as I groaned.

I was dimly aware of calls and doors opening and shutting, of footsteps scurrying back and forth. I recognized the gritty sound of sand pouring down and surmised someone was covering up my vomit. I lay there helpless to move.

"Kill me, Kegleigh, kill me, now. I don't care."

The damp cool cloth that was placed upon my forehead felt like the touch of Heaven. Kegleigh took another wet cloth and cleaned my chin and my mouth with the tender care of a Mother with her babe.

"There's a doctor two streets down.... I've sent for him. Try to sleep now, and no need to worry. You're safe as a lamb."

"Yes, a lamb in a cave of wolves," I thought, closing my eyes. I drifted off to sleep.

"Mistress Henry.... Mistress Henry...."

I woke to a calling voice. It sounded a kindly voice. With an effort I opened my eyes. There beside the bed stood a tall, thin gentleman. His eyes were brown and sympathetic; his black hair tied back with a black ribbon.

"I am Doctor Malbone, Geoffrey Malbone, at your service. Mr. Kegleigh tells me you were taken with a violent illness. I'd like to help. May I?"

I blinked. A doctor? Why did he call a doctor? I'd never been ill in my life. The gentleman took it for granted that I agreed with his request. He laid his dry hand upon my forehead, his touch gentle and steady. He took my arm in his, fingers gently pressing my wrist.

"No fever. That's good," he said. "Might you have eaten something that disagreed with you? Oysters or fish, perhaps?"

I managed to shake my head. My brain felt light but my head no longer ached.

"Are you often taken ill like this?"

"Never," I said. My voice came out in a croak.

"May I have your permission to examine your person? It will involve a little poking and prodding, but it won't take long, I promise."

The gentleman sounded so cheerful that I nodded my assent. Doctor Malbone I'd heard enjoyed an excellent reputation as a physician. The doctor pulled back the bed cover that someone had placed over me while I slept. Malbone was as good as his word. Poke and prod he did, but in a careful and considerate manner. He asked me a few more questions then withdrew from my sight. I closed my eyes to sleep but the tinkling of a glass awakened my curiosity.

Doctor Malbone held out a glass half filled with an amber liquid. "Can you sit up?"

Could I sit up? Of course I could sit up. I chose not to. However, I did not wish to disappoint such an accommodating physician.

"This will soothe the gastric juices," he said, holding out the glass. "I think I can promise that you won't vomit anymore if you drink it."

I raised my head. Doctor Malbone slid a pillow beneath it with one hand while he held the drink to my lips with his other hand. With a little effort, I leaned upon one arm and sipped at the remedy. The taste of mint and sweet woodruff brought relief to my sour mouth.

"There," said the good doctor. "Rest a bit. You'll soon feel better. I'll wait here for half an hour, and then if you've a mind to travel, my carriage is at your disposal. I'll drive you home."

"Home?" The word came out like the mating call of a bullfrog, but I heard it as the sweetest medicine this kind gentleman could offer.

"Yes. Kegleigh agreed that you might prefer to recuperate in the privacy of your own home. I think you'll be up to the journey. Let's just give the medicine a chance to work. I'll have a word with Kegleigh while you rest."

I fell back upon the pillow, overcome by gratitude. A mewling kitten had more strength than I had, but I'd find it in me to crawl through the streets on my hands and knees to get away from Harry Kegleigh. I think I fell asleep. Once more I heard a voice call my name. Good as his word, there stood Doctor Malbone of the kindly face.

"Are you ready?" The doctor's good-natured tone assumed that I was.

Unwilling to disappoint the man, I sat up. The room remained motionless. I swung my legs over the bed and waited for my guts to explode. Nothing. I stood. Doctor Malbone extended his arm and I walked under my own power, even if my knees wobbled like calves-foot jelly. We walked down the hall to the front door. Doctor Malbone held the door open and

I stepped forward to freedom. Drinking in draughts of fresh air, I was nearly overcome with thankful joy. There before me stood the doctor's open carriage, patient nag in harness. The steed looked a veritable Pegasus! The doctor helped me in and I sank back upon comfortably worn leather cushions.

On the short drive across town Doctor Malbone discussed my condition in words of the most encouragement. "You'll soon be your own self," he added. "It's perfectly natural to feel ill upon occasion. Don't worry about it. If I were you, I'd forget I ever met Harry Kegleigh. Oh, he'll stand by you—he stands by his friends, I'll say that for him. It's just that he can be a great oaf at times. Not worth getting into a huff over." He went on to hint that I would be ill advised to call in the magistrates.

I was too tired and too grateful to the gentleman to argue with him. All I wanted was to crawl into my bed and die. The carriage pulled up before my warehouse door. Doctor Malbone helped me down. He handed me his card and bowed low.

"If you have need of me, please send word. I'll come."

"Thank you." I waved as he drove away.

Torches flared bright orange on either side of my front door, a cheery welcome. Home never looked so good to me.

Chapter Thirteen

A full night's sleep and I was back on my feet, shaky but fine. To coddle myself I deemed it best to work at my desk for the day. There is always correspondence to attend to or billing or the books to reconcile. While I employed a clerk to do most of the work, I liked to see for myself how matters were going in trade. Mr. Henry, my second husband, taught me that a fresh eye could spot trends that the daily minutiae of keeping accounts may not reveal.

I enjoy working with figures. I have a knack for it. The necessary concentration kept me from dwelling upon my adventure of the previous evening. It helped keep at bay my anger. I did not want to think of Harry Kegleigh or I might be tempted to take my revenge upon the great oaf. A word in a certain Mohawk's ear and Kegleigh would find his head split by a tomahawk. Friends of my first husband, Jack, would see that Kegleigh received a personal introduction to Davy Jones. I believed in the Biblical admonition, an eye for an eye, but something bothered me. I did not feel in my heart of hearts that Harry Kegleigh murdered Bella Edwards. Perhaps it was the way he held the basin for me, or that he wiped my face with a cloth and acted in such a practical manner. Whatever it was, I felt some confusion about that gentleman. The distraction of the accounts helped.

The parcel came as a complete surprise. I looked up from the accounts book as my clerk carried it into the office, paper-wrapped and twine-tied.

"What is this?" I asked as Paul handed me the parcel.

"A lad brought it for Mistress Henry. I gave him a few pennies and he scurried off before I could question him."

I set down my quill pen and considered the parcel in my hands. "Thank you," I said, dismissing my good Paul. A minute away from the accounts would do me no harm, I thought, so I took out a pair of sharp sheers and snipped away at the string.

The parcel was soft and yielding. Lest its contents slip from my fingers, I set the package upon the desk and pulled back the paper.

Yards of cream lace greeted my eyes. I could not refrain from a gasp of pure pleasure at its beauty, filmy and delicate as fairies wings. In my mind I could picture it flowing from my shoulders and my arms. I heard the whispers of envy from the females of Boston and their inquisitive questions: *Where had I obtained that lace?*

Where *had* I obtained it? I looked for a card. Folded neatly beneath the lace I discovered layers of lustered silk in a soft yellow color that reminded me of daffodils. I fingered the silk with an avaricious touch. Wouldn't this make up into the most sublime gown I'd ever worn? And the lace was perfect for it. With my dark honey-colored hair and green eyes, in my daffodil gown I would outshine every woman in the Colonies. Now who would tempt me with such a vanity?

I could not keep my fingers from the soft cloth, taking bits of it between them and letting the cloth slide through with a sensuous light tug. At the bottom of the parcel I touched stiff paper. I pulled out a white paper, folded and wax-sealed. I broke the seal in unseemly haste. Curiosity has always been one of my faults.

"*To Mrs. Mehitable Henry,*" I read, "*from one who deserves no forgiveness. I leave Friday morning at Seven of the clock for Plymouth. If you will ride out with me from Boston Gate,*

I will answer any questions you may choose to ask me, my word."

The note was signed: "*Your Servant, H. K.*"

Anger blinded me so that I no longer saw the daffodils, only a yellow mist. Ride out with him? Ride out with Harry Kegleigh? I'd as soon keep company with a rattlesnake—at least the rattlesnake would warn before he struck. One rides out with friends, to keep them company for a few miles at the start of a journey. 'Tis a convivial New English custom. One does not ride out with one's enemies whom one wishes at the bottom of the ocean weighted with heavy chains. How dare the rogue! And he needn't think he'd get his silk back, either. I felt under no moral obligation to return his bribe.

And yet the opportunity to question Kegleigh as to his whereabouts upon the night of the murder could not be missed; that was a moral obligation to the community. The killer must be caught.

Creasy could accompany me, and I'd take one of my stout laborers as well. This time I'd heed Creasy's advice. With that resolution I wrapped up the parcel of silks and laces, set it aside and went back to my figures.

Come Friday morning we met Harry Kegleigh at Boston Gate. If he was disappointed in meeting me with my entourage of one Boston minister and a barrel-shaped workman named Iron Dick, he had the grace not to show it. I made the introductions, my voice as chill as the morning breeze.

"I'm glad you've come. You are well?" He tilted his shaggy head to regard me, searching my face.

"I am in the best of health, thank you." I looked straight ahead.

He persisted in regarding me, his black horse sidling next to my mare.

"Am I forgiven for my rude behavior?" He spoke in a low voice. The black horse pranced beneath him but Kegleigh's ham hands held the animal steady.

I could not help but admire the horse. It was a beautiful animal, restive and in want of a gallop. My own mare was a calm sorrel with a sweet ride; one of the Old Snip breed direct from Narragansett.

I shifted my gaze to Creasy and frowned. I hoped Kegleigh took the warning. I had neglected to tell Creasy about my ignominious abduction; I could not bring myself to do it. Besides no harm done to consider.

"Let us not speak of past behavior, Sir," I said. "I am here with my companions because of your offer to answer my questions. We seek the truth, Mister Cotton and I, and we seek justice for a poor soul whose life was cruelly ripped from her body. If you help us with that, why, 'tis to the benefit of your conscience, which may rest all the easier for it."

"I see I must be content with that." Kegleigh gave me a nod and pulled his black horse away.

I told Creasy the note I'd received from Kegleigh was an apology for his behavior. If the minister assumed it was for Kegleigh's kissing me in the warehouse, why I could not help that. Creasy was pleased I'd included him on the morning jaunt, although he thought the guard I'd brought with us unnecessary. After all, he noted, I had the protection of his company.

"I'm only heeding your advice," I'd answered. At which the minister looked pleased. And I did wish I'd listened to him before I'd wandered off into Town to enjoy the evening merriment. It's just that Boston is such a law-abiding place I'd never imagined any harm could come from walking about its streets.

While I knew that Creasy would fight for me if Kegleigh tried any of his tricks, I felt safer with an escort who matched Kegleigh in size and in strength. Iron Dick was noted around the wharf for his feats of strength.

Kegleigh hailed the minister. "How are you faring, Mister Cotton?" He rode his black beast up to Creasy's brown mare.

"Tolerably, sir."

I noted the stiff spine that held Creasy straight in the saddle. Our horses circled around as we positioned ourselves to begin our journey.

"I've heard of your prowess as a wrestler, sir," Kegleigh said.

I turned to regard him. Was he mocking my friend? But Kegleigh did not smile, nor did his lip twitch.

"Wrestling is a skill with which I have some facility," he added

"I wrestled in my youth, sir." Creasy spoke with modesty, waving a black-gloved hand.

"Youth? Why, you are but a youth. How old are you, sir... nineteen? Twenty?" Kegleigh's eyes narrowed, surveying the young minister.

"I have nearly twenty-five years, sir." Creasy drew himself straight in the saddle.

"A mere youth to me," Kegleigh said. He paused, taking the minister's measure. "I would like to meet you in a match, Mister Cotton. I think you would give a good account of yourself."

"You are rather beyond my weight, sir." Creasy raised his black glove in protest.

"Oh, I think you could manage the weight, sir. You've the advantage in reach. Besides, it's a matter of skill, is what I find."

"Last time I wrestled beyond my weight I ended up flat upon my back." Creasy rubbed his head as if it still pained him.

I decided I'd best interrupt before he accepted and did break his head. "If you'd care for a match, I'm sure Dick, here, will accommodate you." My suggestion was ignored by all the men.

"What style do you favor?" Kegleigh quizzed Creasy.

Creasy kept his mare to the black's pace. "I wrestled with the Wampanoag boys growing up, so I learned in the Native style." His face flushed with enthusiasm for his topic. "It was at Harvard that I first became acquainted with the Scottish way. I suppose I have moves from each."

I pulled my horse back to let the two men pass. Kegleigh spoke of wrestling at country fairs in England. My companion, Iron Dick, took in Kegleigh's tales with a look of intense interest.

I let the men rant on about different holds until they began to speak of classic Greek contests.

"By that do you mean they wrestled naked like the Greeks?" I thought my remark amusing. The men did not. Iron Dick's ruddy face flushed an even darker red. Creasy scowled. Only Harry Kegleigh grinned. After more discussion on styles, whether to begin from a standing position, on the merits of a collar hold, I nearly fell asleep upon my mare.

At last I felt it time to call attention to the task at hand. "Mr. Kegleigh," I called out.

The man had the good manners to rein in his black and to wait for my mare to pull abreast.

"Where were you on the night Arabella Edwards was murdered?" I made no effort to lower my voice.

"I was in Ipswich, there on business." Kegleigh was quick with his answer, as if he anticipated the question.

Ipswich is an easy ride to Salem. Kegleigh admitted to being near the scene of the murder. Creasy turned his head to listen to our conversation.

"I have witnesses that I caroused at Sparke's ordinary 'til 'twas long past curfew. Mr. Sparke himself can testify to that as well as can several good citizens of the town, and the night watch, who chased us all to our beds that night." Kegleigh spoke with confidence. "I was carried to my bed, I'm ashamed to say, but in my defense it was Sparkes' own special that did me in."

"Whip-belly-vengeance?" Creasy's long thin brows rose' in a curious look of horror and sympathy.

"How was I to know?" Kegleigh appealed to Creasy.

"Know? Know what?" I frowned. Were they back to talking about wrestling moves? Why couldn't these men be serious?

Creasy called back to me. "Mister Sparke's special drink is called whip-belly-vengeance, and not without good reason."

"I've a hard head for drink, but that...." Kegleigh shook his head. "My companions from Ipswich kept drinking it down. I felt obliged to keep up with them."

The two other male companions of mine nodded their heads in solemn agreement.

I huffed. Was one obliged to drink oneself into a stupor? I think not, but then I am merely a woman. The fact remained that Kegleigh was close enough to the Salem gallows that he might have hung the poor woman. His own words about Bella Edwards flashed into my mind, that she liked to be tied.... I shivered. I had been in this man's clutches, myself. The queasy feeling in my guts returned but I forced it down.

There was no help for it; someone must go to Ipswich and verify the man's statement. While there, we must ask about for a woman of Bella Edward's description. Had she been seen in Kegleigh's company?

"Mister Kegleigh, while you were in Ipswich did you ride over to attend the witch trials?" I asked.

"No, I did not." His answer was firm. "I went to Ipswich on business, I stayed long enough to carouse and to regret it the next morning. Then I took the ferry back to Boston. Why would I want to watch a gaggle of hysterical jades tell tales upon each other? I can't abide such stuff." Kegleigh snorted in contempt.

"Everyone else is interested. I understand there are great crowds. Bella Edwards went to the trials...at least that seems to have been her purpose in going to Salem. With whom did she travel?" I asked.

"If I knew that, don't you think I would go after the man myself? I'd beat him to a bloody pulp." Kegleigh's voice was cold as ice, his eyes glittered like black ice.

Looking into his face, his jaw clenched, I believed him. "Do you know of a blond-haired fellow, a laborer, who fancies himself a poet?" It was a quick change of subject, but I'd not forgotten the young man in the crowd nor his strange poem. As promised, the Town Crier gave me a copy of the verses. The young poet had not been seen since, but the town crier continued to read the verses as he'd been paid to read.

Kegleigh shook his head at the question. "I do not number

many poets among my acquaintance, madam. Why, do you like verses, Hetty? May I call you Hetty?"

"Mrs. Henry." I spoke in a frigid voice. I could not forgive him his treatment of me. Little did he know that at a word from me, he would disappear from the face of the earth. Oh, he'd be alive, but he'd wish he wasn't. There were men of my acquaintance.... I pictured Kegleigh with those great ham hands bloody and blistered as he roofed with the other galley slaves in the far Mediterranean. The image gave me satisfaction.

I pulled upon my reins. The others slowed. "Creasy, do you have any questions for Mr. Kegleigh?"

Creasy turned his mount. "Just one. We found a great deal of moneys in her cash box." He hesitated. "Did she...ah, did she charge you much money for her services?"

Kegleigh's caterpillar brows knit together. "I never paid Bella for her company. Oh, I gave her a jewel now and then, and some amber beads, but they were offered as presents from me, and accepted as such. She never asked me for anything. Bella wasn't a whore, you know. She was true to Edward Ruckenmaul until you people sent him away in chains."

Kegleigh's face was impassive as he spoke. Before Creasy could argue about the graft and corruption that led to Mr. Ruckenmaul's chains, I raised my hand in warning.

"This is as far as we go, sir, a pleasant journey to you." My two companions followed me as I turned my horse away. There was no backward glance for the rogue.

Creasy spurred his mount to ride beside me.

"So...what do you think?"

"He was close enough to the scene," I answered. "He could have done it."

Creasy shook his head. "Even so, I don't believe he did. I couldn't tell you why, except that I saw the look in his eyes when he said he would beat the man to a pulp. I think he meant it. No, I don't believe he murdered Arabella Edwards."

I agreed, but with a sigh of regret. Although I wanted Kegleigh to be guilty—given the slightest encouragement I would believe him guilty—some sense deep down inside me thought otherwise. Oh well, if the man' innocent, he's innocent. There comes a time to set aside unpleasant thoughts and dwelling upon misfortunes. I put Harry Kegleigh out of my mind and clicked my mare into a trot.

Chapter Fifteen

We sat through a pleasant evening of music following the dinner. My companion of the evening, Mr. Boynton, played an oversized instrument he introduced as the violin-cello. A woman in a striped gown played a mellow sounding recorder and a Huguenot gentleman mastered an energetic violin. I did not know the composers of the music but they all had strange Italian names.

Music is not my forte but I was proud when Creasy was coaxed into singing a Huguenot hymn with his mousy dinner companion. She accompanied him in a lyrical voice to his strong baritone. I knew that Creasy had a pleasant voice that he could not show off in church because he was obliged to line out the hymns with his congregation. That is, he led by singing one line and the people would repeat it, off-key. There were times when I'd caught snatches of song from him but I'd really no idea just how well he did sing. I joined in the hearty applause until he took his seat beside me.

"Well done." There was no time to whisper anything more than that before our host stood before the company and regaled us with a cheerful song of his native country. In fact, there was no time to talk whatsoever, once we were seated. The company listened to the music with utmost concentration. It would have been rude of me to converse, except to compliment the musicians and the singers. My eyes closed, my head drooped. The nudge of a sharp elbow in my side startled me.

Creasy frowned down at me, then he turned his head attentively back to our host's duet with the mousy lady. It was a spirited tune, sung in French, and M'sieur appeared to enjoy this duel of musical notes.

I caught myself wondering if the jovial person before me, so helpful to us, was the one who put the rope around the neck of pretty Bella Edward. Why would he do such a thing? How was she a threat to him? Was gold involved? I thought of the unknown poet and the line about Bella's greed for gold. Bella Edwards must have loved gold, for she hoarded it beneath her bed like a miser. But then, jealousy is a strong motive as well as gold. What if Bella rejected Gabriel Germaine for another lover? A rich merchant like M'sieur would not like to be rejected. Perhaps Harry Kegleigh was that other man. I shuddered at the thought.

Ebenezer Boynton, my dinner companion, sat behind the two singers. He leaned slightly forward upon his violin-cello, listening with intent concentration. Would Bella have rejected M'sieur Germaine for him? Boynton's features were pleasing enough but he appeared reserved, his blue eyes cold as ice. Would a seller of hymnals and rare books be capable of gross murder? What possible reason could he have for depriving poor Bella of her life? Had she criticized his hymnals? It was more possible that she dismissed him for the protection of the jolly and wealthy Huguenot merchant. I know I would prefer a man of spirit to a cold fish.

Why did I care who killed the poor woman? It was my duty, of course. As a member of the community and as the wife of a deceased magistrate, I must see that justice prevailed for all persons. Beyond that, I felt sympathy for an unmarried woman making her way in an unfriendly world. An English Rose with the stink of that rotten cabbage Edmund Ruckenmaul about her, she would not find much sun in the thorny

Theology of the Reformed Church. Did I think one of our own church members murdered her for her immoral way of life, as Boynton suggested? No. No one in our community would dare flaunt the law in such a reprehensible manner. The trials of Salem were legal trials, before magistrates of the court, following established procedures. If the outcome was the same, as Boynton charged, it was at least an outcome after due deliberation. So I hope, anyway. I would go to Salem and see for myself, so long as I was there to examine the scene of the crime.

Creasy had obligations to his congregation that prevented him from leaving town immediately for Salem. So he informed me in the carriage as we returned from M'sieur Germaine's dinner. I offered to go on ahead to Salem without him but he insisted I wait for him. I offered to take Iron Dick with me, in his place.

"The Devil is let loose in Salem," he said, his voice grim. It was so dark inside the enclosed carriage I could not see his face. "A strong arm will not protect you against the Devil's wiles. Besides, Cousin Cotton asked me to bring him back a transcript of the proceedings."

"Is he still keeping to his bed?" My scorn must have shown in my voice.

"We must be patient with him, Hetty. It's his nerves—you know he's given to *melancholia.*"

"Don't I know it. Every time he's expected to perform an unpleasant task he falls into one of his bouts and you step in for him. He takes advantage of you, Creasy." I hung on to the carriage strap as the team of grays took a corner. The great hooves resumed a steady clip-clop that was most soothing. The streets were quiet and deserted, most people having retired for the night. An occasional flare of torchlight brightened the street, otherwise it was dark as coal.

Creasy did not answer my observation. I changed the subject. "The hymn you sang was lovely. I know that you have a good voice, but I didn't know you could sing in French. How did you come to learn it?"

'The song is the One hundred and thirty-third psalm. *Assis aux bors de ce superbe fleuve…. Nos tristes cours ne pensoient qu' a Sion."* He recited in a melodious voice. "My father taught me French at an early age. I heard the psalm sung at their services and decided to learn it for my own pleasure. I never thought to sing it in public."

"Well, it was truly lovely," I said. I hoped he could detect my sincerity since he could not see my face in the dark interior of the coach. We were silent for several moments.

"Did you learn anything about Bella Edwards?" I initiated the subject; it was the purpose of the evening, after all. "Your dinner companions seemed to have kept you in constant conversation."

The leather seat cushions creaked as Creasy leaned towards me in confidence. "Gossip, that's all it was. When M'sieur made that toast to Arabella's memory, I asked the ladies about her. Marguerite—that's the one who asked me to sing—seemed more tolerant of her than Joan, the blond English lady."

"How is that?" I murmured, not wanting to be overheard by the carriage driver. "What did they say, exactly?"

"Well, Marguerite said she—Bella, that is—was a woman living alone and must do as she could. Joan called her—Bella—a vixen in heat. Those were her words."

The leather creaked beside me as Creasy shifted in unease. He would not like to repeat such gossip, I knew, but one can learn a great deal from gossip, I think.

"Marguerite said she had the sense to be in heat for men of wealth but Joan claimed that Bella slept with her footman. It was all gossip, Hetty. I could not learn anything of substance. I'm sorry." He leaned back in the carriage.

I couldn't expect him to see gossip as a useful tool, or as a means of loosening someone's tongue.

"I didn't do much better, I'm afraid," I confided. "My companion, Ebenezer Boynton, knew Bella Edwards in London, before she came here with Edward Ruckenmaul. And I only found that out through Mr. Hacker, who was silent most of the evening. Mr. Boynton sells English Chapel hymnals…and rare books," I added. "Perhaps Mr. Hacker can tell us more about him, if he will. I think we should speak to Mr. Hacker again. If it does not concern Bella's business interests, perhaps he will be more forthcoming with us."

I leaned back against the carriage seat. Although I maintained my hold upon the strap, I did enjoy the luxury of traveling by coach. I knew several people in Boston who kept coaches but the vehicles were of little use beyond Town. Should I attempt to go by coach to my farm in Rumney Marsh, the wheels would get stuck in the muds of spring, sink into the hard ruts of summer and skid in the ice of winter. I thought of Doctor Malbone's light carriage, open with only a top to keep out the weather. I thought of Doctor Malbone. I did not tell Creasy that I'd ever met him, but he'd been introduced to me just before dinner. He'd greeted me with a cheerful countenance, bent over my hand, and passed on. Only the slightest pressure upon my palm reassured me that he would maintain discrete silence about our prior meeting. I'd looked around for him at the musical interlude but Geoffrey Malbone was not present. Perhaps he'd been called away to a patient. There was another person who might prove helpful in the search for Bella Edward's killer.

I closed my eyes, shifting with the gentle sway of the carriage. The soothing thuds of the giant gray hooves were the only sounds in the night. I must have dozed off. I thought I was having a nightmare, at the first. I felt as if my body was propelled through space by some malevolent force. The crack of my head against the coach roof woke me to reality. The carriage swayed at a perilous angle as I tumbled to the floor. I slid into a bundle against the carriage door. The bundle cried out. My head felt as if a tomahawk were buried in it; I could not see a thing but I heard curses, shouts, creakings and clankings and the frightened neighs of horses. The coach jounced up and down, wreaking havoc upon my poor brain-pan. Someone cried out in pain but I could not tell if it was me or the knee that I clutched upon the floor.

My name I heard, but I had no breath to answer. The coach jiggled up and down so that I felt sick in my bowels. At the same moment I tried to call out to Creasy. Where was he? What if he were injured? What if he needed my help? I forced myself to reach up for the coach seat and grasp its comforting leather. In doing so, I leaned against the leg beside me—was it mine?—for there came a loud moan of protest as I dragged myself to my knees. I rested my cheek against the soft leather and waited for my senses to assert themselves through the throbbing of my noggin. Curses worthy of a seaman mingled with creakings and stampings as the carriage jerked this way and that. It was time for prayer, I realized, and I prayed mightily for the commotion to stop even as I clung to the leather seat with the talons of an eagle. I did not dare move my head.

"Hetty?" A voice, groaning, called out my name.

I could only croak. Without lifting my head from the seat I forced myself to take a deep breath. I swallowed. Again I heard my name and sought to respond: "Yes."

"Are you hurt?"

"Hurt?" Well, if having a tomahawk sticking out of your skull was hurt, then I was hurt. I didn't dare loosen my grip upon the seat to check upon my limbs or my nether regions. For all I knew an arm or a leg might be missing except, of course, I could feel my knees hard upon the floor and I did have both hands embedded in the leather here. There was some kind of comfort in the puffs of leather beneath my fingers; in the musty smell of dead cow that seeped into my nostrils.

"My leg...it hurts. I can't move," the voice said. Its words were clipped. "Are you injured?"

"Bump," I said.

"Yes, the coach almost tipped. I'm pinned against the door here."

"Bump...bump."

"Yes, we must have bumped something. Are you injured?" The words were spoken between gritted teeth. He was impatient with me. I gave up.

"No," I said. And after all, perhaps this was just temporal pain, pain that would ease when the angels came to lift us to glory. As if in answer to my prayers a bright, shimmering light filled the carriage window where my eyes were turned. I had to close my lashes against its brilliance. Had angels indeed come to take us from this Vale of Woe? Were we about to join with The Elect? Oh heavenly bliss, when our earthly pains would fall away from us, when our souls should shed their sins lightly as feathers! Oh Rapture!

The light framed a florid face with reddened eyes and ruddy cheeks. I felt my soul shrink inside me. Oh, were we Judged and found wanting? Was this The Prince of Darkness come to carry us down to the blasting fires of Eternal Damnation? Oh Woe! I knew in a flash a thousand sins upon my soul that brought me to this dreaded state. But Creasy...my companion...a Man of God! What had he done to deserve this? Did my sins doom him, as well?

"Madam...madam...are you harmed?" The voice came from the window. Was I harmed? Of course my sins harmed me. Did he want a confession? I noticed the nightcap upon the florid head. How silly of the Evil One to wear a nightcap. We must have caught him unprepared.

The voice beside me called out, "I'm trapped here!"

Yes, we were trapped...trapped by the consequences of our own loathsome natures! And the man beside me trapped because he befriended me. Oh, Woe!

"Take heart, sir," the Spectre said and withdrew his face. The light continued to flare.

Fires of Eternal Woe, I thought, but the Spectre went on that he would have us out in a trice and not to fear. Satan's voice seemed to come from all directions. Wily serpent, of course he would have us in his horrible talons and carry us down.... The carriage door opened and a fiery torch thrust its way into the coach, the upper body of the head in the nightcap behind it. If I closed my eyes it might go away. But I felt the hand of Satan upon me and his words rang in my ear.

"Come, madam, let me help you to descend."

Descend? Descend willingly to the Fires of the Damned? I attempted to pull away but I had no strength within my limbs.

"My wife will see you safe, madam. There's nothing to fear. Come," the man coaxed. The wily serpent with his soft, kind, enticing voice…I could not resist. Satan in his silly nightcap took my arm and handed me down from the coach into the stout arms of his wife, the Queen of Hell. She, too, wore a nightcap. And a shawl over a nightrail. She clucked like a mother hen. Satan's wife felt round and soft and comforting. I leaned gratefully against her, I could not help it. A softer road to Hell than I envisioned…who would have thought it? She led me down the primrose path. I only turned back to look for my companion and witnessed his poor body being handed down from the coach upon the shoulders of two stout gentlemen, one of whom wore a nightcap.

"Don't fret, mistress, my good man and our good neighbor will see to your husband. You just come into the house and we'll see to your injuries." The Queen of Hell made soothing clucking noises as she supported me forward.

Fortune smiled upon us, Creasy and I, for our injuries were minor. Painful but minor. I had a bump upon my head and a small cut upon my forehead. Creasy's leg was beginning to swell—it would be black and blue by morning—but he could limp upon it. He'd thrust it through the floor boards. A salve of plantain applied to our bruises and an infusion of burdock root to drink restored our outer and inner selves. The poor coachman remained with his horses, refusing to leave them. A tankard of beer was brought out to him. His curses had pierced the sleep of the neighborhood and brought immediate help. There had been an accident, as I surmised even with my sore head. I did not want to think on it; all I wanted was my own bed. Our kind hosts offered us shelter for the night but as we were only streets away from my rooms, I declined. Creasy must have felt the same. Our hosts provided us with two mounts and a guide, to make sure we made it back in safety, which we did.

The next morning I fond myself with a spot upon my head sore to the touch, but only if I fingered it. My hair covered the spot. I felt no worse for the prior evening's accident, a good night's sleep having cured my aches and pains. *There is no reason why I shouldn't report to my office as usual*, I thought. *There are papers to sign, entries to record, clerks to consult before I leave for Salem.*

My first duty was to send a basket of fresh strawberries, just up from my farm in Rumney Marsh, to our rescuers of last night. To think I'd mistaken the kindly couple for the Dark Prince and his Queen! My brainpan must have been shaken like calves-foot jelly. I could not help but to reach up and touch the sore spot, wincing as a result of my foolishness. Then I penned a note and sent it off to Creasy, to let him know that I'd recovered nicely and how was his leg? Courtesies accomplished, I called for my business ledgers.

The note my clerk brought in to my office caught me by surprise. I'd forgotten that I'd asked the Harbor Pilot to inform me when a young girl named Edwards appeared on the passenger lists of English vessels. The terse note read: *Edwards, girl-child of nine years, The Lion, Captn. George.*

I dropped my pen and scurried out of my office, the note still in my hand. The passengers would disembark soon; someone must meet the poor mite. If I'd had advance warning, I would have arranged for Creasy and perhaps Esther Thripenny to accompany me to the wharf, but there was no time now.

The usual chaos surrounded the dock; a babble of shouts and cries, milling passengers searching for displaced trunks, stripe-shirted sailors pushing their way through the crowds, burly laborers lugging cargo from the hold, busy clerks poking and tallying bundles, checking off lists. I approached one of the clerks who stood by a pile of trunks.

"A girl-child on board the Lion; one Mistress Edwards?"

The clerk slid a long quill down a sheet of paper. He

nodded. "Disembarked."

"Where is she?" I asked.

The clerk shrugged.

I glanced around the dock. Two boys ran around and through a pile of trunks and boxes. The boys dodged, hid and chased each other, as boys will. They might be more apt to notice a young girl than a busy clerk would, I thought. I approached the pile of trunks.

"Hi," I called out. The boys stopped in their tracks. I stepped up to address the bigger boy of the two. Wharf rats, thought I, holding my nose at the smell. Dirty and tattered clothing, knit caps over greasy locks…wharf rats. The wharves draw such boys like bees to flowers.

"Did you see a little girl of about nine years, just come off *The Lion*?"

"What's her name?" The big boy stepped in front of the other, hands upon his hips, a challenge in his voice.

"Her name is of no account to you," I said, scowling at his impudence. "Mind your manners. Did you see a little girl of about nine years or not?"

The smaller boy ducked around his companion and faced me. His knit cap hung over his face and I could see beady eyes glittering beneath the fold. He reminded me of Ferret; a made a mental note to pay my young spy another visit.

The tatterdemalion had the audacity to glare at me.

"Are you my mother?"

"Am I your…?" I gasped aloud at the creature's effrontery.

"Are you my mother, yes or no?" The creature stamped its over-large boot.

"Most certainly not!" I drew back my shoulders. I must track down its parent and have a talk with said unfortunate about teaching respect for one's elders and betters. "Why, what is your name, you rude boy?" I questioned.

"I'm not a boy." The creature pulled off its cap and a tangle of dirty hair of indeterminate color tumbled down its back.

A dreadful suspicion seized my gut and clenched it tight

into a ball. "What is your name, child?"

"My name is Celia Edwards, and I'm a girl." The creature spoke in a calm voice.

I stood nonplussed, staring at the ragged child before me.

"Did my mother send you to meet me? Where is she?"

I did not know what to answer. Where is Bella Edwards, in Heaven or in Hell? I suspected the latter, but that was not mine to judge, for which I felt thankful. Still, the truth is always the best course, and the child would have to know sooner or later.

"Your mother is dead, child. Better you should know…." I stammered, afraid the child would fuss. What would I do if it started to whine and blubber? I felt most unprepared for this encounter.

The creature's sharp eyes bored into my own. It did not look like a child who whined and blubbered.

"I can't go back to Aunt Meg in London. She doesn't have room for me, what with the new baby. Where shall I go, then?" The child was all practicality.

I must say that I approved this attitude. "Why, you must go to your mother's house," I said. "There is a housekeeper—she can take care of you."

The child nodded. What a relief to find her so reasonable! But I could not present her to the public like this, with soiled smock and ragged trousers, serviceable because they were made of sailcloth, but soiled beyond boiling. And she smelled like a dead eel. I held my breath even as I extended my hand to her.

The child placed both her hands behind her back. "You have not introduced yourself." She frowned up at me. "Are you a friend of my mother's?"

I felt irritation rise at the child's audacity, but she had the right of it. In my astonishment at finding her in such a state, I had not introduced myself.

"My name is Mrs. Henry. I never met your mother in life, but one might say I became her friend in death. A respected personage of this town, a minister of the church, asked me to look out for you." Cousin Cotton Mather would certainly insist that I look out for this child. Cousin Cotton was very good with children; a more tenderhearted parent did not exist. "Come, where's your trunk? I'll see that it gets carried to your mother's home. But first you may change your clothes—and wash," I added, "at my house."

The child turned, shook her companion's hand with a solemn leave-taking, and ran to the pile of luggage. She returned with a dirty canvas bag.

"Where are your clothes?" I asked.

"This is my dress. I only have the one. William, there, sold me these clothes so I wouldn't get my dress too dirty." She waved to the larger boy, who waved back with a grin. "William's a sailor," she explained.

I shook my head and took her grimy hand in mine. On the short walk to my warehouse I questioned her about her lack of wardrobe.

"Aunt Meg needed my clothes for the other girls," she said, her face cheerful. "She said my mother would give me all the pretty dresses I want. Only I don't want dresses. I like these sailor clothes better. I ran all around the ship, and no one bothered me because I looked like a boy. It's better to be a boy."

I did not bother to correct her. She seemed like a child of spirit; she'd learn soon enough how to use the fortunes God has bestowed upon us as women. As we walked I planned out what I could do. One of my clerks had a large family of daughters; I could beg some clothing for my waif—I'd make it worth their while, of course. And as soon as the child was properly fed—children are always hungry, I know that much of them—and washed and clothed, then I could present her in public. First to Mister Hacker, for it was almost certain the child would inherit the house and a great deal of cash. As Arabella's business agent, Hacker would know the figures. I'd pen a note to old Esther. What a surprise awaited her! How would she react? She would have continued employment taking care of the child, if she chose to remain. And I'd have the opportunity to see Ferret, my observant young spy. What had gone one at Casa Bella since that lady's death? I'd be interested to learn who visited since the news became public. All in all, the child's arrival upon our shores promised a lively time.

I was prepared for the whines and protests of the bathing process; I was even prepared for the task of burning her old clothes, none of which were salvageable, and prepared for her protests when I made her put on the robe and apron loaned by my clerk and his good wife. Celia Edwards proved a handsome child, slender and straight of carriage with blue eyes of bright intelligence and hair as fine and blond as new corn silk.

Our first stop was to the seamstress, where I discovered the child had a particular stubborn opinion when it came to colors and fabric. We argued over serviceable russet wool over the pale lemon silk I favored; over lace trim for the apron, which she rejected, over caps and gloves and ribbons, none of which she approved. What was I to do with such a child? Let old Esther have her and welcome, I decided, as I dragged her from the shop.

"The streets in Boston have strange name," she observed as we made our way to Mr. Hacker's office. "Fish Street...Cow Lane.... What other animal streets do you have?"

"This is foolish," I grunted. "Cow Lane is where the cows were taken to pasture in the old days and Fish Street...well, that's where the fishing boats dock. It's obvious."

"What other animal streets do you have here?" The child was persistent.

"Well...there's Mackrell Lane, Black Horse Lane, Green Dragon Lane...."

"Oh, I should like to see a green dragon!" the child interrupted, skipping up and down. "Can we go there?"

I sighed in exasperation. "There is no green dragon to see, you foolish girl. It's only a tavern."

"Can we eat there? I'm hungry. I want to eat at the place with the dragon." She pulled upon my hand, dragging back.

"Mind your slippers," I said, pulling her along. The slippers fit her little feet; my clerk's wife had thoughtfully included them in a packet of clothing.

"I want my old boots. I paid William for them."

What a rebellious child! "I'll pay you for them and we'll make a present of them to some needy little boy. It's good to be charitable." The child must learn the ways of Boston.

"I'm hungry. Why can't we eat at the green dragon place?" She pulled once more upon my hand and I once more dragged her forward.

"Because we are not near the Green Dragon Tavern, that's why. We're going to see a man who knew your mother very well. He needs to know that you are here."

"Well, where is this dragon place? Tell me that, then."

"Do you see that big hill with the tower upon it?" I turned and pointed to Sentry Hill." At her nod, I went on with simplified directions before I turned the conversation back to Mr. Hacker. "This gentleman takes care of your mother's money; he will see that you have food and clothes and whatever else you need. It's important that we talk to him. I will introduce you, then you may wait outside by the street, so long as you don't wander off." No need for the poor child to sit around while Hacker and I thrashed out business details.

Mr. Hacker looked over the rim of his glasses at the child while Celia leaned her weight upon me and yawned.

"Looks like her mother."

His words reassured me that I would not have to prove her identity in a nasty legal fight. I handed him the two papers I had in my possession, including the letter from Arabella's sister. As he perused the papers, Celia tugged upon my hand.

"I'm hungry."

"Hush," I said. "Go outside now. Mr. Hacker and I have business to discuss, as I told you." I released her hand and Celia scuttled sideways to the door.

Every time I tried to ascertain the amount of Arabella

Edward's estate, Mr. Hacker withdrew like a turtle into its shell. Nor would he tell me whether the former secretary of the provinces, Edward Ruckenmaul, made any provision for either Arabella or her child. Attempting to make the man see reason, that his client was dead and her privacy no longer mattered because of the child's need, exhausted me beyond measure. The best I could do was to offer to provide for her myself should Arabella's funds dry up. That brought a snort that I interpreted as amusement at the thought. "So the child was indeed provided with enough funds that I need not worry," I asked? And he gave a grudging nod.

A good hour or so passed before I stepped out of Mr. Hacker's office. I fully expected a sullen and angry child to confront me and guilt at my negligence nagged my conscience. Children could not help feeling hungry, even though I'd fed her bread and cheese before her bath. The poor tyke had nothing but ship's fare for the past four weeks; she needed good meat and fresh vegetables for her small frame. I'd take her to the nearest ordinary or tavern, or even find a pie cart and reward her patience.

There was no little girl in sight, angry or otherwise.

"Celia Edwards," I called out. "Child, where are you?" Two men stopped to stare at me. How exasperating the child was! I told her to stay by the office door. Perhaps she'd ducked into one of the warehouse shops across the street. I marched across and peered around or poked my head through the doorway in search of her. Merchants shook their heads at my questioning. No little girl with blond hair had invaded their shops. I crossed once more and stood before Mr. Hacker's doorstep, my face hot, my blood up. When I caught hold of that child I'd give her a good shake. Play her little tricks on me, would she? I looked down to see my foot tapping upon the dirt. Where was the naughty thing? Where could she have gotten?

I didn't dare venture from the doorstep lest the child come back and find me gone. What would she do then, the little minx? It would serve her right if I did leave her. Let Mr.

Hacker take her to her mother's house. He'd enjoy that, no end. Perhaps she'd tried to find her way there without me! But she didn't know the address, nor would most people in town know where Bella Edwards lived...my head began to ache, the result, no doubt, of last evening's adventure. The teetering coach flashed through my mind. What if the little thing had run into the street and been run over by a carriage? What if, even now, she lay bleeding in the street somewhere, no mother to comfort her, no one even knowing her name! My guts churned; I could not breathe. Where was the constable when you needed him?

I glanced wildly around. Why had I left her for so long a time? Why had I brought her to this place? Why had I not sent a note to Creasy to meet us here? Surely she would not have run away with him around; he had a way with children. How he would scold me because I'd lost the child! What kind of woman was I to lose a child in the streets of Boston? I should have taken her directly to Arabella's home; I should have placed her in old Esther's care immediately. Yet how would Esther Thripenny have received a dirty smelly little girl in boy's clothing? I clutched my head to contain the pounding. I must ask Mr. Hacker for help....

There was a carter coming up the street; I'd ask him to go for the constable. I took a step into the street and raised my hand to stop the man. Then I spied a laborer turn the corner one street down. His bulk at first hid the little girl whose hand he held. The man saw me, bent to the child, spoke to her, pointed in my direction and released her hand. She nodded, waved and came running towards me.

"Celia!" My eyes filled with the moisture of relief. "Thank the All Mighty!" I grabbed the child and pulled her into an embrace. She held still, bearing it. "Don't ever do that again!" I released her and stepped back to examine her. "Why you might have been run over by a cart...whatever possessed you...? Oh, never mind. I'm just glad to find you safe."

The child looked up at me with eyes that sparkled like blue lakes. Her cheeks were flushed with color. "I'm sorry for not minding you, Mrs. Henry," she recited. "I shan't run off without telling you again. The nice man said I must tell you that," she added.

"Yes, well, the nice man is right. I'll just thank him for his kindness in restoring you to me, and we'll be on our way!" I looked up and down the street, but the laborer was nowhere to be seen. "A pity," I said. "I would give him something for his pains."

The child tugged upon the edge of my shawl. "Can we get something to eat, please? I'm hungry."

Chapter Seventeen

As we rode towards Salem Town I told Creasy about the unexpected appearance of Arabella Edwards' daughter and how I'd brought her to Esther Chandler, upon the advice of Mister Hacker—advice given with a grudging tone of disapproval, I noted. On the way I'd stopped to introduce her to my little spy, Ferret. The two youngsters took an instant dislike to each other, especially since Ferret informed Celia that girls couldn't be members of the Young Spies League. Celia pointed out that I was a girl, and I was head of the Boston organization. Ferret counted with the fact that I was an old lady, not a girl.

Creasy chuckled as I recounted the puppy fights. (I thought it best to forego the fact that I'd lost the child on my way to taking her to her new home. He would only lecture me on my carelessness, and the child had returned in safety, after all.)

"How did old Esther receive her?" Creasy asked, his interest plain.

"She looked petrified," I answered. Indeed, only my reminder that the house was now the child's property and Esther would be able to stay on as housekeeper stopped her whining that she was too overworked to be looking after a child, what with her household duties and no one to help her but a simpleton.

At this point, I thought it politic to apologize to my companion for neglecting to inform him of the child's arrival, but I'd had no time. "The child was there, waiting upon the dock," I explained. "I had to dispose of…place her in a home before we left for Salem. I couldn't let her go to the workhouse, after all." I knew Creasy would agree to this sentiment, although the workhouse is clean and warm, with sufficient food for the indigent widow. Still, it was not a home for children. Creasy, with his warm heart for little ones, acquiesced at once.

"And how did the child feel, left in the care of a stranger in a strange land? Poor little mite…she must have been weary and frightened." He cleared his throat with a sympathetic cough.

I looked over at him. "Celia Edwards?" I made a most unladylike snort. "That child can take care of herself. It's poor old Esther who's frightened. As soon as the child walked in she took over the house. She must see every room and cry out 'This is mine. And this is mine. And that bed is mine. And that chair is mine. And that great thing with the shiny plates upon it is mine.' And when I scolded her for her vanity she answered me: 'Well, Mister Hacker said so.' Oh, don't worry about the child. Esther has her hands full, I can tell you." I shook my head.

"I will say that the child has a generous nature." I added this to be fair to Celia Edwards. I didn't want Creasy to get the wrong impression of her. "She asked me if her Aunt Meg and the children could come live there with her."

Creasy cleared his throat in a hum of approval. "What did you say to that?"

"I said she must speak to Mister Hacker." I shrugged my shoulders. "It is he who knows the amount of her inheritance. He would not share that information with me." That man's tight-lipped disapproval of my inquiry rankled with me. Had I not delivered the child to him? Was I not investigating the matter of the mother's death? Was I not a merchant of good standing in the town? Here was I, carrying on the commercial ventures of my two late husbands, and he felt he could not trust me. I'd kept more momentous secrets than the paltry sums of the mistress of a Crown official. My companion interrupted my brooding.

"It would seem an excellent idea for the aunt to come live here with the child. I don't like the thought of her being left with only an old woman for protection," Creasy said, his brows lifted in worry. "Don't forget there is a great deal of money in that money box beneath the bed. It may be a sore temptation to others besides the murderer of Arabella Edwards. I hope the child is safe."

"She has Joseph and Ferret to call upon." I was quick to assure the man. The thought had caused me some worry, as well. "I asked that young scamp Ferret to keep an eye out for her, and she knows she can run to his house if there is any trouble. He'll hide her, he promised me. And there is Joseph— he's a strong young man, even if he is simple, and he's devoted to the child all ready." I was confident of the child's safety and I wanted to reassure Creasy of it. Celia had charmed Joseph as soon as he laid eyes upon the child. She'd walked up to him and taken his hand and introduced herself. And if Ferret argued with the girl, it was because he felt himself a superior male whose job it was to protect the weaker vessel.

"As for the moneybox, Mister Hacker will collect that for safe keeping, and so I told Celia. She is to accept a receipt from him and hide it in a safe place. Indeed, she and Ferret nearly came to blows as to which one could find the best hiding places." My words seemed to relieve Creasy.

Thinking of my shifty little spy, I related his report upon the comings and goings since Arabella's death became public.

"Ferret saw Mister Hacker come up the hill twice, he says. At least the boy described the horse as Hacker's. Each of the other men came once and the Huguenot came in his coach with the grays. He had a lady in the coach with him. I wonder who that was."

Creasy began to speak but I continued on: "Oh, and there were two men who walked up the hill. One of them I believe to be Esther's son—he came three times—and another man came once on foot. Ferret could not describe him but said he was a laborer of some sort. Esther confirmed the visits, and the neighbors came for the funeral cakes and meats."

Creasy raised his hand in a motion to still my tongue. I nodded.

"Speaking of M'sieur's coach, I have some news to tell you," he said.

"It seems the blacksmith discovered a cotter pin missing from one wheel. The coachman insists the pin was in place earlier in the day. Perhaps it loosened somehow or perhaps someone pulled it loose…just enough so that it would work its way out and cause the wheel to fall off."

I looked over at my companion. His expression was serious, his lips compressed.

"Surely it was an accident?" I tend to be hopeful.

"The blacksmith was of the opinion that it was pried loose. There were scratches around the hole. I don't want to think it, Hetty, but we've been asking very many questions about a certain woman of ill repute."

"Could someone be after the Huguenot? M'sieur must have enemies. All people of wealth have others who envy them. And he did have to flee France, after all. Perhaps it's someone from his past. I shall make inquiries about him," I said. I had excellent resources for information about my competitors. As a woman among male merchants I found that certain information served me well.

"I won't offer you false comfort. You wouldn't want that, Hetty. We were the ones who used the coach that evening," Creasy pointed out.

"Is Harry Kegleigh returned to Town?" I asked.

"Even if he is, how would he know we were riding in M'sieur's coach? He wasn't at dinner. But many other people were…and we were seen arriving in the coach."

Creasy wrinkled his nose in distaste at my obvious jump to a conclusion, but he didn't know my reasons for wanting Kegleigh to be the villain. I didn't intend to tell him unless I must testify under oath. It was too embarrassing.

"Coaches!" I could not help a sigh. The mishap in that

coach cured me of my sins of pride and vanity in desiring one of the vehicles. Just because it was new and showy, I had to have one. That it was huge and cumbersome and dangerous had not mattered to me...until it had tipped over on me. I rubbed the sore spot upon my head. How weak are we humans in our desires! I pondered upon my sins all the way to Salem.

Ingersoll's tavern is the center of Salem village life. It is the meeting place town for town government, for weary travelers, for a congenial evening with friends. Nathaniel Ingersoll and his wife Joan are the hosts who welcome all with cheerful demeanor, courteous service and rare discretion. This tavern, a steep-gabled building, was the site of the original site of the witch trials until the crowds of the concerned and the curious overflowed its hall and the court of oyer and terminer was moved to the larger structure of the meeting house across the green.

The Ingersolls were the obvious choice to question about Arabella Edwards. If anyone knew about the woman's time in Salem it would be either Nate or Joan.

We stepped into pandemonium when we opened the door. Fearful screams met our ears, crowds of people pushed and shoved towards the great hall, a rumble of angry male voices added to the commotion. Creasy raised himself up on tiptoe.

"What is it? Is there a fire?" I grabbed his coat sleeve in alarm. What if we had to make a hasty retreat? I heard male voices shout: "There it i! No, over there! There! There!"

I tugged upon Creasy's sleeve. "What is it?" Fire spreads rapidly and did horrible damage. It was always a danger in our homes and often women's clothing caught sparks from the hearth fires. What if a serving girl's apron had caught fire? Those screams were high-pitched and youthful.

Creasy glanced down at me, uncertain. "I don't think its fire. I don't see any smoke. All I see is a man poking in the air with a sword, that's all I see."

I was bumped up against him as more people entered the

room and shoved their way towards the screams. Grabbing my companion's coat to keep myself from falling and being trampled, I looked around and spied the staircase. Perhaps I could see something from that point, although it led away from the hall. I forced my way over and climbed the steps. I discovered that if I leaned over the banister and twisted my body I could see into the right section of the hall. I could make out an arm in a green-sleeved coat wielding a sword that he thrust into the air with a jabbing motion. I heard encouraging screams in female voices: "There...there...you've chased her up to the beam! There she sits, Goody Nurse, and a yellow bird sets by her!"

I could make out the beam but there sat no good woman nor did any bird perch in my view. One voice rose above the rest: "Oh, oh, she pinches me! She pinches me!"

Other voices chimed in with a chant: "She pinches me, she pinches me!" This chant was accompanied by a stamping of many feet in unison. A young woman in a white cap and collar leaped up within my sight, her hands clutching her throat. "Oh, she chokes me! She says I must sign her book! Oh, no, no, I will not sign your book!" The young woman's eyes rolled back in her head, she gasped for air, her tongue protruded like a snake from her mouth. Spittle dripped from her chin, her arms flailed wide. She fell from my sight.

The chorus chanted out: "She chokes me! She chokes me!" The sound of many feet stamping upon the floor beat a loud tattoo. Men voices rose into a roar. The noise bored into my brain so that I felt dizzy. I unwound myself and sat down hard upon the step.

Creasy took the stairs two steps at a time. "Are you ill?" He bent over me.

I nodded. "They are calling out upon a woman, aren't they? They accuse her of being a witch?"

Creasy put his hand upon my arm as if to give me courage. "Ho, Landlord! Landlady!"

I heard him call out as a wall of black obliterated my

senses.

Chapter Eighteen

I woke up to find myself fully dressed upon a bed in an unfamiliar room. The face that greeted my eyes was that of Joan Ingersoll. She held out a mug of steaming liquid. I raised myself up on my two arms to receive the mug. Two large hands thrust a pillow behind my back as I moved; Creasy straightened his lanky frame. He looked as agitated as a mother hen.

"Don't fuss." Even to my own ears I sounded waspish. I don't like people fussing about me. To make amends for my rude tone I turned my head and summoned up a smile for the gentleman. "It's nothing, don't worry. I'm just tired from the journey. You would insist upon traveling by horseback, after all." Creasy did not like to travel by boat unless it was a necessity, as I'd discovered. Me, I never get seasick.

I took the cup from Joan's hands and sipped. The scent of lavender wafted pleasurably into my nostrils. I drew in a deep breath. I looked down into the mug; the pale green liquid eased my dry throat as I sipped. "What is it, violets and dandelion greens?" I asked.

Joan nodded.

I gave my own nod of approval. This was a good spring tonic, healthful and strengthening. I drank the infusion willingly.

Joan turned to the gentleman who stood vigil over me. "I'll look after her, Sir. Mrs. Henry will be restored presently, you may be sure. Why don't you go below and watch the proceedings?" Her smile dismissed Creasy as surely as a command.

I waved my own hand to enforce her dismissal. Creasy turned at the door, his eyes upon me, but I waved him through. There were questions I wished to ask Joan and they were best asked as two women confiding in each other. No doubt Joan had questions for me, as well, and I wondered if I could put this intelligent woman off as easily as we'd put Creasy off.

First I finished my mug of spring tonic, sipping slowly at it so that I could organize my thoughts. I handed Joan the empty vessel.

"What's going on here?" I patted the bed beside me, inviting the woman to seat herself. She did. With her in close proximity I could see the tired lines creasing her face. Her fair blue eyes were red-rimmed. In all the years I'd known Joan Ingersoll I'd never seen her less than calm and cheerful. I felt a stab of fear in my gut. If Joan Ingersoll was thus affected, the situation in Salem Village must be desperate.

"Madness," she signed aloud. "Madness. That's what's going on. It affects all who enter our village. I suggest that you tarry here no longer than is necessary for you, Hetty." As she spoke, she turned the mug around in her hands, absorbed in matters that I guessed were of far greater import than its round shape.

"They were crying out upon someone downstairs, isn't that what all the screeching was about?" I asked. Tiny goose bumps sprouted upon my arms as I spoke. I knew what devastation a charge of witchcraft could bring to a town. "An old woman, is it?" In my experience old and feeble women were the usual recipients of such charges, if only because they were wise in the wicked ways of the world and unafraid to challenge those in higher authority.

"They cry out on everyone...the old, the infirm, the hale, the hearty, persons of good standing, beggars...everyone now." Joan screwed up her lips and her pale brows in disgust. "Charges are laid by those with grudges, and they do it through the girls. Even if the maids wish to retract—and some of them do want to retract their charges—the magistrates will not let them. The magistrates see devils all around them. They let the devils speak in court and will take the word of a ghost over that of a valued member of the community. Only Satan wins out in Salem." Joan lifted her head to meet my gaze. I saw a challenge there, as if she defied me to report her to the magistrates. I would never do so; perhaps she saw that in my eyes. She lowered her head. We sat there in silence for a moment. Then she looked up with a different kind of gaze, one of shrewd speculation, and I dreaded that look more than the challenge.

"Now, what ails you, Hetty? You gave your young man quite a fright, fainting like that upon my staircase." Tired eyes searched mine.

"He's not my young man," I said, catching at the phrase in objection. He's Increase Cotton, Uncle Increase Mather's nephew. That's who he is. Creasy…Mister Cotton…and I came to Salem to look into the matter of Arabella Edwards' death. She's the one was found hanged next to the witch…to the convicted witch. Cousin Cotton Mather sent us, as he himself is indisposed. He suffers from poor health, you know. This matter in your village much troubles him, adding to his nerves, so Creasy and I have offered to look into the death of Arabella Edwards. At least we can relieve him of that worry." No doubt I sounded defensive in her ears but I did want to correct any misconception concerning my relationship to the young minister. There has been enough talk about us as it is. "You may have heard that Mister Cotton and I have had some success in solving similar crimes… Well, all such crimes are unique and vile to God and to Man, but Creasy and I have a particular talent for finding the truth of them. And that is the Lord's gift," I added.

Joan seemed only mildly interested in our talents, however. Worry lines etched creases across her forehead. "Oh," she said. She pushed a stray strand of hair back beneath her crisp white cap.

"Did you see the woman here, Joan? Arabella Edwards, that is. Did you see anyone that might have been her?" I swung my legs over the side of the bed as I spoke and settled my skirts about me. No matter that I'd blacked out upon the stairs, I felt no ill effects from sitting up.

Joan only gave a slow shake of her head. "There are so many come, you see. So many strangers come into this tavern now...new ones every day. We have no more rooms. The sheriff asked us about her but we could tell him nothing. Poor woman, if she came here we did not notice her."

"Do you know a man named Harry Kegleigh? A great blustering brute of a man. You would remember him, I'm certain. He stables a handsome black animal. Was he here?"

But Joan only shook her head. Nor could she confirm my descriptions of the features of Messier Germaine or of Mister Boynton. She had not noticed any of those men in the throngs that entered her tavern. I felt disheartened. Bella Edwards dressed in unobtrusive clothing. She would blend in well with the crowds come to gawk. People remarked upon her golden hair, but she would have covered that feature with a hood, at least in public venues. So, I wondered, who might have seen her without her hood? Who might have seen her in a private setting? Besides her killer, that is. I asked Joan's permission to question her servants. Surely Bella and her companion had stopped for breakfast or dinner at some point. Perhaps they'd come in for a glass of ale or cider. Perhaps the servers had caught a glimpse of that golden hair as they brought food or drink to the table. I had no doubt they would remember a great bull of a man like Harry Kegleigh. M'sieur Germaine they might remember by his accent, although he spoke English very well. Mister Boynton they might possibly remember as a polished gentleman, although his features were unremarkable.

I waited until the accusations were over for the afternoon before I descended and sought out Creasy. The shrieks and stampings, the stink of unwashed bodies and manured boots— an honest smell, for all that—were not conducive to questioning. Creasy and I took a table and ordered our dinners. I told him of my conversation with Joan and that we might look to the servants for answers. Creasy began to question me about my health but I put him off. Or rather the arrival of a loin of veal with caper sauce demanded my attention. He seemed to relax as I dug into a generous portion with my usual zest. I spooned a helping of new spring peas on to my plate, adding a good amount of boiled onions, which I then passed on to my companion. Ingersoll's golden cider sparkled all the way down my throat in copious draughts. When I finally set down my spoon and my tankard my companion leaned forward over the table.

"The poor children were sorely afflicted, Hetty. I am glad you weren't there to hear their pitiful cries and laments. It was a dreadful thing to behold."

"Children?" I stressed the word with incredulity. "Creasy, those children are maids of marriageable age. What they need are husbands and infants to keep them too busy to make mischief. That's what they need."

Creasy winced and motioned with his hands for me to lower my voice. I had been rather loud. Fortunately the volume of diners and drinkers had drowned me out.

"They have red welts on their arms, Hetty. You can see them, the marks are visible. The poor girls say the devil pinches them. It is pitiable, Hetty, truly pitiable."

I could not believe what I was hearing. Well, I could believe it. Creasy was as trusting as a baby, especially where women were concerned. It was not odd that he had been taken in by the young maids. Their cries were horrid and frightening. I myself had been unnerved by their unearthly screeching, but that was because I sensed the danger behind the laments. Suspicion, hard words, fright, debts, accusations—I had seen their cruel effects in my own town of Rumney Marsh. One poor old creature had been accused of witchcraft and the mob had turned upon her. I must refresh Creasy's memory.

"Old Gammar Pisspot was accused of murder by

maleficium and she died for it, yet she was innocent of the charge. These maids are fomenting the same madness, don't you see that?" I asked. "As for their bruises…why, they may pinch themselves and no one the wiser. Joan Ingersoll says they have packets of pins in their pockets and have been seen to make use of them in the courtroom. You are too easily taken in, Creasy. Leave this for the magistrates to sort out and let us get on with our own task of questioning the servants."

Creasy mumbled his reply.

"What's that? Speak up, man!" It annoyed me when he mumbled like that.

"I said I shall pray for them, just the same."

"Pray for those they accuse," I said. "They will have need of your prayers."

We rose from our seats. The crowd had thinned by this time and the maid behind the bar's grate readied clean mugs and glasses for the next influx of customers. I stood back and let Creasy bestow his charm upon the maid. She could not remember seeing anyone of Bella Edwards' description in the tavern. I stepped in and offered a monetary reward for information, knowing it was the fastest way to spread word among the servants. The bar maid gave us the address of three other taverns that took in guests. "What with so many new people coming in to Town we cannot accommodate them all," she said. Two other of Joan's servants had no new information to add. There were just too many people coming and going to remember them all. We received the same response in three other places.

I was standing outside the third tavern waiting for Creasy to bring the horses around when I felt a tug upon my skirt. I turned and almost missed seeing a tiny gnome of a creature. She wore a drab, shapeless garment beneath an apron stained in splotches of green, orange and brown. She smelled of sweat and onion and she might be of any age between eight and eighty. Matted hair of indeterminate color hung over her face but two bright sparrow eyes peered up at me.

"Miss…excuse me, miss…." The creature's voice was high

pitched and hoarse.

"Yes?" I peered down at the little person. She shifted her tiny feet in scuffed boots. The sparrow eyes blinked. She did not speak.

"Don't be afraid," I said. "You wish to speak to me?"

The little person nodded.

I examined her with a bit of skepticism in my mind. Who was this little person? She appeared to be a kitchen maid but we'd not interviewed her with the other servants of the house. Why had she not appeared with the others? What information could a scullery maid have? Busy with the hearth fires and implements and the pots and skillets, what contact could she have had with the guests of the establishment? The little creature flushed under my scrutiny. Oh well, thought I, any little bit of information was better than none. I reached out and took her hand, smiling down at her to reassure her I meant her no harm.

"Come, what have you to say to me? Mister Cotton has gone for the horses. We will be obliged to you for any help you may give us." I pressed the cold, rough hand within mine. "Do you prefer to wait for my companion so that he may hear, as well?"

The little person shook her head with some vigor. She cast an anxious glance around and would have withdrawn her hand had I not held it safe. The sparrow was ready to take flight.

"Then you may speak freely to me...as one woman to another, then." There are women who feel most comfortable confiding in another woman; I took it the little sparrow was one such.

"We came in search of information about the woman who was hung next to the witch...." I did not like to refer to the poor victim as a witch, although she had been tried and executed as such. However, this is how the local people viewed her. "This poor woman was cruelly murdered. Mister Cotton and I were sent to find out who killed her. Her name was Arabella Edwards."

The little person bobbed her head up and down. "I was hiding behind the wash tub," she said, in a whisper. "I heard that man ask the others. He was angry."

"Creasy...Mister Cotton? He wasn't angry, he was just frustrated. Do you know what that means?" I gave her hand a squeeze of reassurance.

The little person looked up at me with wide eyes. "He has a big voice."

"Well, he is a good man, a minister in Boston. He needs to have a big voice so that his congregation can hear him when he speaks. We have asked so many people about Mistress Edwards and no one can remember her—that is why he sounded angry to you. Can you tell me anything about her?"

The little person nodded, again with vigor.

"She was here? Here in this tavern?" I felt a quiver in my gut. I wrapped her small hand with both of mine. She would not run away from me. "Are you sure it was her?"

The little person stammered her answer. "Her hair...gold...like gold coins. That's what they said of her...she had hair of g-gold. I knew it was her." The little person gulped in a deep breath of air. She straightened her shoulders and looked straight into my eyes.

"There was no one else they could send, you see. Missus Lumley give me a clean apron and said I must bring a tray up to the Rose Chamber. Everyone was busy serving meals, there was that great a crowd. I carried up the tray and the lady opened the door for me. That's when I saw her hair...gold, all around her shoulders, like the sun. Oh, it was lovely!" The little person's eyes shone at the memory.

"Go on," I urged.

"She gave me a coin and took the tray from my hands. She said nothing but she smiled at me.... Such a nice lady! Oh, she had no boots on. She was in stockings of silk, with clocks on them." The little person added this in a matter of fact tone. "I noted this because her robe was of plain striped material like what Miss's Lumley might wear. I just noted it, that's all."

I was impressed with her powers of observation. "Did you

see the lady's companion?" I held my breath, hardly daring to hope our search would be rewarded with a description of the killer. The little person before me was the first person who'd given me any hope at all!

My informant pursed her small mouth. "No, but he was there."

I grip tightened upon the little hand within mine until I had to recall that I might be hurting her. I'd no wish to do such a thing. The little person seemed to understand my anxiety.

"She said nothing to me, but when she closed the door I could not help hear her words. She said: 'Here's your dinner, Froggy. Now perhaps you won't be such a scold!' I thought perhaps it was a funny kind of a pet for a lady, but then a man's voice answered. I couldn't hear what he said, but it was a man's voice. Isn't it peculiar to call a man Froggy? That's a funny kind of a name, and so I thought. And that's what I wanted to tell you, Miss. Miss's Lumley wouldn't hear me. When the sheriff's man came I was too frightened to speak, but you seemed like a kind lady. Maybe it's not the same lady that was hung...I hope it isn't, but I just had to tell you."

The little person took a deep breath after this long speech. I gave her hand a final squeeze, bent over to kiss her cheek and then I found a coin in my pocket which I presented to her with my—and Creasy's—deepest gratitude. I told her my name and discovered that her name was Susan. I told her to contact Mistress Ingersoll at Ingersoll's tavern if she had any further information for me,

"What you've told me is very important, Susan. If there is anything I may ever do for you, I beg that you will call upon me."

The little person curtsied and scurried away. I shifted my feet, turning my head this way and that, impatient for Creasy to appear with the horses. Important? Bella Edwards had a habit or the caution to give her friends nick-names. Which one was Froggy? Find that out and we'd found our killer!

Chapter Nineteen

All the way back to my farm in Rumney Marsh we argued as to the identity of <u>Froggy.</u>

"It must be Harry Kegleigh…a great blustering fellow with a loud voice like a bull frog," I argued.

But Creasy shook his head in doubt. "M'sieur Germaine has the stout, round shape of a frog and he is French. It's just as possibly—in fact it's more probably—that he is Froggy and not Kegleigh. I don't mean to accuse M'sieur, you understand. There's also Boynton, the bookseller. From what I've heard he's quite the…." Creasy paused, choosing his words. "Wooer, shall we say. The man's as amorous as a bull frog in the spring. So it's just as possible he may be this Froggy. Or it could be some other man we have yet to uncover."

"It's Kegleigh. He admits to being at Ipswich—he could easily have ridden over to Salem."

Creasy guided his horse around a stump in the path. A moment later he spoke. "Well, I don't intend to argue with you." Creasy proceeded to lecture me about keeping an open mind, adding thirty reasons why Froggy could be anyone but Harry Kegleigh.

It was with relief t hat I parted form the man, he to return to Boston. I had farm matters to attend that would occupy me for several days. While I employed an extremely competent and honest manager, it never does to let a man make all the decisions. My farm exerts a powerful draw for me. There is something soothing in the smells, the mud, the cackling critters underfoot, the green shoots in the fields, the sweat of planting, the pride of harvesting what you grew. There were also memories of a comfortable, loving second marriage here. My memories of my Mister Henry fueled my determination to find the murderer of Arabella Edwards. Hezekiah Henry was a magistrate with a compelling sense of duty. The welfare of the community he carried upon his broad shoulders, a burden Mister Henry accepted with extraordinary grace. Could I do no less?

Perhaps my methods differed from my late husband—well, I was no magistrate—but we saw our duty as the same. Especially with the horrors of Salem spreading to other towns, it is more than ever essential to see that justice is carried out, even for the poorest members of our society. Even for those followers of the former Royal Tyrant, Governor Edmund Andros, who would have taken our liberties and our justice away from us.

After three days of pulling weeds in the fields, I was a sight to see. I wore an old striped smock over ragged petticoats which I tucked up beneath a belt of rope, with my husband's oldest boots upon my feet and an old bonnet upon my head. I stopped to wipe the sweat from my brow when I saw three pairs of astonished eyes peering over the hedgerow. I scrambled up from my knees and made a futile attempt to remove the clods of dirt off my smock. "Gentlemen...." I gestured to the end of the row.

Three bewigged heads nodded and bobbed like fluffy white cats above the green. I met them where the hedgerow ended and the field began.

"Have you come about the pigs?" I asked, pulling my petticoats down as I spoke. Then I recognized two of the men; the Rumney Marsh constable and the magistrate. I wiped my hands upon my dirt-stained smock. It flashed through my brain that I must look like the lowliest of servants, all sweat and dirt. This thought was confirmed by the pursed lips and knotted brows before me. Well, pulling weeds was hard work but it must be done and I was not above doing it. I pulled off the floppy bonnet, which I wore to shield my neck and head from the sun.

"There's a fine litter in the sty." I pointed toward the barn. "You couldn't find healthier piglets anyplace. Strong and fat...guaranteed to produce the best hams you've ever tasted. Everyone knows the quality of Priscilla's piglets." I stepped forward to lead the gentlemen to the pig sty.

The magistrate, Nathaniel Saltonstall, held up a fine-boned hand. "Mrs. Henry, may we have a word with you? Up at the house, perhaps?"

"Certainly," I said. I gathered up my skirts and led the three men through the garden to the farm house, entering through the ell into the kitchen. "Go on through into the parlour, gentlemen." I directed them through with a dirty hand. "I'll be with you in a moment."

I sent the servant girl with cider and cakes while I dashed up the back stairs to my room. A splash of cold water from the basin cleared my befogged brain and a swipe with a sudsy cloth removed the stains from my brow and cheeks and hands. I drew my smock over my head and dropped it on the floor; the petticoats followed. I pulled out a fresh white petticoat from the chest and rifled through the highboy for a plain fawn-colored linen gown to wear over the petticoat. There was no time to fix my hair so ran a brush through it, pulled it back tight and tied it behind my neck with a black silk ribbon. A new lace cap set upon my head and I achieved a respectable appearance. I walked with as much dignity as I could muster down the front staircase and into the parlour, where the gentlemen were still drinking their cider.

The three men leaped to their feet as I entered the room. I held out my clean hand to Mister Saltonstall, something I had not dared to do in the field, and nodded to Tom Pengry, the constable.

"It's good to see you, sir," I said to Mister Saltonstall. He took my hand and squeezed it with a gentle pressure as he bowed. I noted the flush upon his face and the beads of sweat that clung like tiny raindrops upon his forehead.

"It's rather hot out, isn't it? Please, sit down, gentlemen. Finish your cider," I urged. The poor gentlemen looked as if they were the ones who just came in from the fields. To put them at ease I seated myself upon a straight-backed chair. I helped myself to a glass of cider from the table between us, pouring from a large white pitcher. The gentlemen continued to look in distress, Tom Pengry fingering the white band that drooped from his neck, but they fell back into their seats, two upon the settle and the magistrate in a chair like my own.

I was mystified by their silence. The magistrate I knew as a colleague of my late husband; a simple, affable man of good family. Pengry had once worked as hired labor upon the farm.

"I don't believe I have the acquaintance of your companion, Mr. Pengry," I said. The two sat beside each other upon the hard wooden settle. Pengry cleared his throat and raised inquiring brows at the magistrate. I'd never known him to be short of words before.

Mister Saltonstall answered me. "Mrs. Henry, this is Jeremiah Coffin, assistant to Mr. Pengry, here."

Coffin bent his head with a shy, solemn nod while Tom Pengry's ruddy face grew scarlet.

Mr. Coffin was a lanky, lean gentleman dressed in a threadbare bottle green coat. He wore wide-legged canvas trousers over striped stockings and I guessed that he had been to sea at some point in his life. I turned my attention back to the magistrate. Obviously this was a formal visit of sorts.

"How may I help you, gentlemen?" I leaned forward in my chair, inclining my head. I would help the officers of the law in any way I could.

Nathaniel Saltonstall rubbed long fingers together. "Damnable business, ma'am, damnable business. We've come from Salem, ma'am." He paused.

I felt a stone harden in my gut. "Salem is a damnable business," I agreed.

The kindly magistrate placed the tips of his fingers together, like an arrow pointing at me. A kind of numbness spread from the stone throughout my innards. "And what has brought you from Salem to my farm?"

"I'm sorry, ma'am—damnable business, as I say. I've been sent to question you, Mrs. Henry." The long fingers rubbed delicately against each other as he spoke. "There's been a deposition taken against you, ma'am. Woman named Sarah Stiles. You know of her?"

My brain froze in my head but I knew the name. I was able to nod at the magistrate. Sarah Stiles was an officious old busy-body in Rumney Marsh. Her husband was a selectman, a poor farmer whose only productive crop was the marsh grass that grew on his land. Sarah thought herself above the other good wives of Rumney Marsh and she never made secret her belief that my Mr. Henry had made an unfortunate choice in marrying me. I was after his money, she told everyone in town, as though I hadn't been left a fortune with the capture of a Spanish galleon by my late first husband, Jack.

"The woman charges that you...well, that you traffic with Satan. She says that she saw you."

The cold fog spread through my body; my limbs could not move. Perhaps it was a dream? I tried to shake myself free of the numbing sensation that threatened to overcome me. It would not do to faint, not now. I needed all my wits. I forced my mouth to move.

"The woman is mistaken," I said, my throat dry and the words coming out as a croak. My ears buzzed.

Good Mr. Saltonstall regarded me with anxious eyes. He rubbed his fingers over and over.

I took a deep breath. "What does the deposition say? May I see it?" I must know what my enemy charged before I could refute it.

The magistrate only shook his head. "I will read it to you, if you wish."

His tone was one of sympathy, which brought me a small measure of comfort.

"Because of your position, you see," the magistrate went on, "we are allowed to question you here, at your home. This is preliminary testimony, you understand...."

At least I was not to be dragged off to the overflowing jail, like so many other poor wretches. The jail in Salem was now so crowded the overflow was sent on to Boston, there to be shackled in chains and displayed for the amusement of the Town. Neither accommodation appealed to me. "Read me the deposition," I said.

"Mistress Sarah Stiles, good wife of Rumney Marsh, on this day in June..." The magistrate began to read from the paper in his hands, his voice low but clear. "Let me see...we shall pass over the formalities, I think, and get to the meat. I am sure you would prefer that..." He glanced over his wire-rimmed glasses for my approval.

Oh, by all means skip the formalities, I thought to myself. *What good are the words that authorize your hanging?* I remained silent, however.

"Ah, here it is. This is the heart of it, Mrs. Henry. *On the twenty-fourth day of February in the year of Our Lord 1692, I, Sarah Stiles of Rumney Marsh, walked to the farmhouse of Mrs. Mehitable Henry, wife of the late Hezekiah Henry, hoping to purchase a basket of flour from the widow, the Stiles pantry having run short of said grain and Mrs. Henry's flour being of a particular fine quality....* Well dear me, so it is!" Saltonstall looked up from the paper. "I've often said so myself. Your flour is of excellent quality."

If the gentleman thought to encourage me with this praise it failed in raising my spirits. I thought only that Sarah had come begging, knowing I would not turn her away nor accept payment for the means of making her daily bread. She was not above begging, my neighbor, but she'd turn around and swear out a warrant to arrest me. I had no words to answer the magistrate. The two men beside him continued to look uncomfortable and strained.

Mister Saltonstall went on. *"As I neared the Henry's barn I saw a strange tall man in a black hat and cloak being admitted into her house by the back door. Not wishing to disturb Mrs. Henry while she entertained her visitor I lingered outside the kitchen window...."*

I'll just bet she did, the nosy gossip! Anger began to burn through the fog of my mind at this picture. Spying on me, I'll be bound, so she could run around to her neighbors and spout her lies and make charges that could lead to my death! Consorting with Satan was a crime of the most heinous sort! *Maleficium* meant the gallows for certain. I forced myself to pay attention as the magistrate went on reading his paper.

"The shutters were pulled shut and I could not see in but I heard strange noises inside of growls and sounds of fierce animals and in short order I heard the howling of a wolf so unearthly that it raised bumps all over my skin and I was sore afraid! I knew then that it was the Man in Black, that Satan had turned into a wolf and no sooner had this knowledge overcome me but the devil came after me in the shape of a wolf who snapped at me and showed his ferocious teeth. I then ran down the path to the gate and shut the gate fast so the wolf could not reach me, only gnash his horrid teeth at me as I ran down the road in fear for my very life! Signed and witnessed this day...." The magistrate lowered the paper. "Well, you can understand why we must question you, Mrs. Henry."

I was unable to answer him for the moment. A lump as big as a...well, a frog, prevented me from talking. I could feel my face burning but I could not help that, either. Yet I must answer the charges. I cleared my throat three times.

"The woman is mistaken, as I told you. I did have a visitor about that time—a gentleman from Albany. You must know that I have business interests in that colony. He came to pay his respects to me, finding himself in the Boston area. That is all." I spoke with as much calm as I could muster. "As for the rest, it is her imagination. If she indeed saw a wolf, why it must have been after my stock. I have no idea."

The magistrate leaned forward, brows raised in interest. "A foreign gentleman, you say? From the Dutch colony?"

"The Dutch dress in a different manner than we do," I

said. "She has mistaken the gentleman. I believe he is a member of the Dutch Reformed Church, baptized in Christ much as you and I, sir. It is not right to slander a church because its members may dress in a different manner. I certainly do not entertain the Prince of Darkness in my home, gentlemen, and I resent the charge that I do." I began to feel quite put out as I spoke. "Perhaps you should go back to the woman who makes such ridiculous accusations and question whether she is mistaken in her mind. Why does she wait so long to report what she now charges? Ask her that, will you?" I flung the question out as a challenge. Slander me, will she? If the penalty were not so serious I could almost feel pity for the woman. But Salem brought a madness into the community that defied wisdom and sense. I rose from my chair, indicating to the gentlemen that our interview was at an end. The three men slid off their seats and stood in a solemn line.

Magistrate Saltonstall tried to placate me, saying I could answer the charges in court, but I had no intention of placing myself at the mercy of a pack of she-wolves. The magistrate informed that I must confine myself to my farm for the present, until such time as the court would consider the charge against me. The poor man tilted his head, regarding me in pity. It turned out that Mr. Coffin had been appointed to keep guard over me, but that he would stay outside the house itself. Mr. Saltonstall requested sleeping space within my barn for the man, and to that I must agree. The sheriff merely stood by and looked glum. Mr. Coffin stood silent and grim.

"I am under house arrest, then?" My spine stiffened with resolve. I would find out what was behind the charge. I would do whatever I must to keep my freedom, on that I was determined. The gentlemen took their leave with sidewise shuffling steps that were almost apologetic. A moment later I peeked out the kitchen window to find that Mr. Coffin had taken up his post outside the house.

I slumped down upon the bench before the hearth, but not even the warmth from the fire could take the chill from my bones. Here I was under house arrest and all because William Blue Bear paid me a mid-winter visit! Blue Bear wasn't exactly Dutch but he did come from Albany to see me. We did have business interests together...and other interests. And he was baptized in Christ, for his Mohawk mother was a Christian. Blue Bear's father was a leader among his people, much respected for his wisdom. William could read and write and was educated far beyond me. He was also an astute man of business. I respected him for that, and for certain other qualities. Sarah Stiles' claim was not too far from the truth. William Blue Bear, the Mohawk, is considered a veritable Satan in certain quarters—the French in Montreal for the ferocity of his raids against their settlements; by the Eastern Indians who fell beneath his war club. Yes, he is a devil when aroused, as I have cause to know. I closed my eyes and reveled in certain memories.

Blue Bear upon my doorstep all dressed in black...no wonder she had mistaken him! Black wool cloak, black breeches, black stockings, black cap, all of which clothing he'd torn off as soon as the door closed behind him. Most of my own clothing disappeared under his ministrations and I had felt the full force of Blue Bear's mighty war club. That was when I'd thrown back my head and howled. It's a good thing the shutters were closed against the winter cold or Mistress Stiles would have gone blind at the sight. Who could have known what two people can do on a straight-backed chair?

The hearth fire did not warm me but those memories did. If they thought I was going to let myself be carried off to a cold filthy jail they were sadly mistaken. I had too much to live for.

Chapter Twenty

The pounding eventually penetrated Creasy Cotton's concentration. He paused, quill pen poised like the sword of Damocles over the sheet of parchment. Yes, there was an appalling sound coming from...the door, yes, his front door. It wasn't unusual for a minister to be summoned from his sermon for an emergency of some kind, and at any hour. And the hour was? Creasy twisted in his seat and peered across the study into the hall. The clock stood tall and proud there, its arms moving to the Roman numerals that meant nine o'clock. Not so late in the evening, yet an inappropriate time for a social call. Who could be at his door at this hour? Death bed calls usually came at three or four in the morning; accidents and injury calls from about six in the morning until sundown, when all good people were safe at home after the day's labors. At six in the morning farmers came in for the market, their carts cumbersome and heavy with produce. Foot traffic increased, merchants opened their shops, sailors thronged in from the wharfs, horses and coaches clogged the narrow lanes, apprentices ran about their business, children and animals dodged about like water bugs—it's a wonder that he was not called out half the day!

The young minister set down his quill. A blob of dark ink promptly dripped from its edge plop onto the scripture he'd just written out for his sermon on Sunday. The ink slithered like a black serpent across the holy lines: *Psalm 22:2: O my God, I cry in the daytime but thou hearest not.* The text had been especially chosen. Creasy groaned aloud, reaching for a piece of blotting paper, half rising from his chair as he did so. The insistent pounding upon his front door proved a weighty distraction from a weighty topic. He turned his gazer to the door, then to the paper, then back to the door. In an act of defiance he flung an old shred of blotting paper over the ink and rose, knocking over his chair in the process.

Creasy strode to the front door and flung it open. He barely had time to catch and to shore up the ragged lad who fell against him. The lad mumbled words too low for him to hear. He held the boy up with one arm and closed the door with the over. Who was the poor lad? Not one of his congregation or he would have known his identity at once. Was he injured? They would come to him because he would treat them for free. Ministers must treat the body as well as the soul, a fact he quickly learned once he left Harvard College. Creasy saw no signs of blood; he took it for granted that no bones were broken. The boy who leaned against him was clearly exhausted; no doubt he was famished as well. In his experience, boys this age were always famished. And they stank.

Creasy wrinkled his nose. The boy's coat was old, frayed and too big for the small frame. A dirty knit cap hung over the lad's eyes. Canvas trousers appeared to be held on by a rope; Creasy saw dirty ends flopping down beneath the coat. His shoes were bulky, scarred and several sizes too large, judging from the shuffling gait as Creasy led him down the hall. The boy smelled of dead eels. A cabin boy from one of the ships docked in the harbor? A fishmonger's apprentice?

No matter. The lad sought him out and he would do his best to help.

Creasy shouldered the boy into the kitchen. The hearth lay in embers but he would stir them up for a bit of heat. Creasy set the boy down at the drop-leaf table near the hearth.

"I'll get you some cold meat and cheese." Creasy kept his voice cheerful to encourage the lad. "We'll have a talk after you've eaten something. Rest there for a moment while I fix you a plate, will you?" Perhaps the lad worked on a ship, living on a diet of moldy meat and weevil-infested biscuits. He certainly looked scrawny enough to be near starvation. So many lads ran away to sea these days—and regretted their rashness when the first swells hit. He'd reunited more than one homesick lad with his family. Perhaps he'd a tale to tell of beatings and abuse on the high seas. There was precious little Creasy could do about that, except perhaps to find the boy a softer birth with a kinder captain.

Creasy removed a leg of lamb from the larder. He busied himself cutting off thick slices of meat, adding a good chunk of cheese and a small bowl of crimson strawberries to a wooden platter. He thought to himself how fortunate it was that Hetty Henry had provisioned him before he'd left her in Rumney Marsh. He'd come back to Boston with a huge, heavy basket strapped on to the saddle. His larder was not usually so full. His congregation of poor widows and sailors had little to spare for their minister's keep. There was the odd jar of mint sauce, a squash or a fruit pie in season, but when Creasy felt hungry he usually sent out for a meat pie or walked around the corner to the tavern there.

Creasy turned, the platter in his hands. He nearly cursed in vexation. He sighed aloud, caught himself, and pulled in his lips until he looked like a toothless old man. The lad slumped there in his chair, his head upon the table, audibly snoring. Creasy set the platter back in the larder. He took a deep breath and tip-toed across the floor. Best to make up a bed by the hearth and let the boy sleep.

For the second time in the week I opened my eyes and found myself in a strange bed.

I found myself blinking at the sunlight that flooded the small room. What a plain, spare place, I thought, with no bright bed curtains or canopy to soften the room. The bedposts stuck up like spikes hammered into the wood frame of the bed. I pulled my arms from beneath a threadbare coverlet of light blue and stretched. What was that dangling up there? Where were my hands? I felt a sudden stab of anxiety. Had they cut off my hands for the crime of *mali fecium*? I shook my arms and my hands popped to the surface from a long sheath of white linen. There they were, all five fingers safe on each.

"Good. You're awake."

I turned at the voice, my gaze passing over the familiar features to the tray held in two long-fingered hands. I spied a bowl of ripe crimson strawberries, a white pitcher of milk and slices of thick, crusty bread. My insides gurgled aloud in pleasure. I did not care if my hunger was audible; I reached for the tray.

"I thought you might be hungry." Creasy handed me a large square of linen before he relinquished the tray into my grasp.

I set the tray upon my lap and looked up at the man towering over me like an angel of mercy. "In bed?" I inquired. "I'm to eat in bed?" It seemed sinful. I was not an invalid, after all.

"Eat," he answered. "It's permitted."

I poured frothy milk from the white pitcher and dug into the bowl of strawberries with a pewter spoon. When I set down the spoon inside the empty bowl, I turned my attention to the bread, breaking off chunks and stuffing them into my mouth. All I'd had for sustenance in the last two days was a mug of ale and four hard ship biscuits. Everything on the tray tasted like manna from Heaven.

I mumbled my thanks to the angel who'd delivered me from want. He provided me with even more manna in the form of a dewy glass of cider. I sipped at the amber liquid, proud of my restraint. I could have gulped it down my gullet in one draught. After I'd drained the glass to the last sparkling drop, I set it with care upon the tray and turned my full attention to my host.

"Creasy, what am I doing in your bed?" I could not remember coming to this point. Of course, the last two days I'd been on the run like a deer hunted by a pack of wolves. I knew that I sought a safe place to hide, but this gentleman's bed wasn't in my plans.   I'd best hide *under* it, not in it. I looked up at him with raised eyebrows.

"Mehitable Henry, will you do me the honor of becoming my wife?"

I shook my head, wondering if I'd lost my hearing or my wits. Increase Cotton stood by the bed as straight as a stork, his hands clasped together in prayer. Whether he prayed for deliverance from his rash proposal I knew not; I only knew that my face was on fire. I could feel an awful sense of doom flood my being.

"Oh, Creasy, has it come to that? Did we...?" I could not go on.

Creasy frowned and shook his head. "No...no...it's not that...not at all! You need a husband, Hetty. And I want to marry you," he added. "It's no sacrifice at all. It would be an honor. Indeed, it would be...an honor." He hesitated, shifting from one foot to the other.

The poor man looked so alarmed I took pity upon him, my own anxiety much relieved.   I lifted the tray and handed it to him. He set it upon the nightstand with a clatter of bowl and glass. I propped the pillow up behind me and leaned back.

"How do I come to be wearing your nightshirt, Creasy?" Curiosity overcame my reluctance to broach the subject. I was no longer alarmed by the possible answer.

Chapter Twenty-one

Creasy was so horrified at my tale of facing a charge of witchcraft that he forgot to lecture me on my other predicament. Not that his lectures would've made any difference. Those plans had not been made without every consideration—except for marriage with Increase Cotton as a solution. That was never in my plans. And it still wasn't, although I appreciated his proposal no matter how desperately offered.

I concluded my story with my fortunate escape from my jailer. "Poor Mister Coffin. He was so certain I would never get past his eagle eye... There the man was, patrolling the yard as proud as a goose."

"What did you do?" Creasy leaned towards me, all eyes and ears.

Did I detect a touch of foreboding in that lean face?

"Oh, I brought the man a fish pie for his dinner, that's all." I could not keep a certain smug tone from my voice.

"A fish pie...." Creasy hesitated, tilting his black head at an angle. "Priscilla?"

I nodded. "That's her favorite treat. I usually make extra for her. She can smell fish pie a mile away. When Mister Coffin took his pie and sat down on that stump by the barn... you know the one, Creasy. Anyway, Priscilla came barreling around the corner, squealing like a rusty wagon w heel. Coffin took one look and nipped off across the yard as if Satan was at his heels."

I don't know whether the sound my companion made was a suppressed laugh or a moan, but I continued with my tale.

"Last I saw of the man he was crashing into the reeds. Poor fool...if only he'd dropped the pie, Priscilla would've stopped in her tracks. But no, he still had the pan clutched to his bosom when he disappeared from my sight.

I thought the look Creasy gave me was quite peculiar.

"And you just happened to have your horse saddled and ready, I suppose," he said.

"Well I can't very well find out who killed Arabella Edwards if I'm stuck at the farm with the threat of a noose hanging over my head. Someone knows that," I pointed out. "Creasy, you have to go to Rumney Marsh and talk to Sarah Stiles. Find out who put her up to this. She didn't think of it on her own, I'll be bound. Find out who paid her—I know her greedy bones. The woman would sell her own mother into slavery if someone offered her money for it." An unladylike snort escaped from my nose. Sarah Stiles is married to a man to whom misfortune sticks like a burr. Malachi Stiles either plants too late or too early; rain clouds either pass by his fields or drown them; raccoons and deer beat him to harvest; but the true misfortune of his life was marrying that woman. Her mouth drips honey to your face but as soon as you turn your back, venom pours forth like a rattlesnake strike. But I dishonor the rattlesnake, who at least gives warning to its victim.

"And another thing," I added. "Find that little kitchen maid, Susan, and ask her if she's heard anything else about Froggy. Take care with her, she's skittish. You'll have to use a soft voice. Tell her I sent you to speak to her."

Creasy ran a hand over his sleek head. (Creasy wore his hair pulled back and tied with a ribbon. Not for him the fashionable periwig of his cousin Cotton Mather.)

"Yes, I'll go," he said. "I have to give my sermon on the Sabbath but I can leave on Monday morning. I'm sure Mister

Willard won't mind keeping an eye on my flock."

When I observed that we were about Cousin Cotton's business and that he should oblige Creasy, my companion replied at once.

"Oh, of course Cousin Cotton would oblige... no doubt about it. It's just that my congregation feels more comfortable with Mister Willard...and South Church is closer to us, after all." At my look of skepticism he went on: "Well, you know Cousin Cotton...he speaks in wonderful similes but his words are difficult for my church to grasp. Mister Willard is a plain-spoken man."

I nodded, understanding. *'The jewel in the Ethiope's ear'* was a pretty conceit but not one likely to appeal to a congregation of poor laborers, sailors and widows.

"Well...." I pushed back the covers. "It's time I was up and about my business."

Creasy rose to his feet. "No...no...stay in bed. No need for you to get up just yet, Hetty. Rest, why don't you? You should stay in bed yet a while." He spread out his fingers as if to make me stay in place.

I waved a shirtsleeve at him. "I can't stay here. This is the first place they'll come looking for me. They know we're working together, asking questions about Arabella Edwards. The constable is bound to come question you, and it's best if you don't know where I am. That'll be the truth. Oh...you may tell them that I was seen boarding my ship. I made sure I was seen getting on board the Anhinga—that's where I got my clothes. The Anhinga sailed from port, but the cabin boy didn't." I shook back my sleeve and beckoned to him. "Now bring me my clothes, if you will. I must get dressed. There are people I need to contact."

But Creasy shook his head. "No one saw you come here—not in those old rags. You're safe enough, and you really should rest. You were so tired last night...."

"Yes," I interrupted. "And I've had a good night's sleep. Thank you. Now if you'll just get my clothes, I'll be off."

My host looked perplexed. He turned both palms up as if

to appeal to me. "But...but...really, Hetty, you should keep to your bed another day at least. All that running around...it can't have been good for you. Perhaps I should send for the doctor?" He cocked his head like a robin listening for a worm in the ground.

I took pity upon the man and didn't curse him out. "I've seen a doctor, Creasy, and I'm perfectly healthy. I promise I'll send for him if I feel the slightest twinge of discomfort. I shan't take any chances in that respect, I assure you."

I thought of Doctor Malbone and of meeting him in the home of M'sieur Germaine. He was a friend of Harry Kegleigh, yet I'd trusted him. What did I really know of Geoffrey Malbone? I felt certain of his professional ability, but as friend of Kegleigh was I wise to trust him? How well did he know Arabella Edwards? He must have known of her, either from Kegleigh or because they moved in the same circle of King's Chapel adherents. Doctor Malbone was a man worth questioning, if I could find a way to do it without making my presence known to the constables or to the Salem sheriff.

"Where are my things?" I glanced around the room but couldn't see a pile of rags.

"What things?" Thin black brows rose in innocent inquiry.

"My clothes. What I wore when I came in. Where are they?" The man wasn't usually so dense. I'd borrowed the clothes from a young seaman. The idea I'd borrowed from Celia Edwards. I must admit that the disguise proved very effective. I walked the streets of Boston without attracting any attention. Young sailor lads were a common enough sight in Town. Even Creasy hadn't recognized me in boy's attire.

Hetty, those rags were so filthy...I couldn't even pass them on to the poorest of my congregation! And they smelled like dead eels. I'll walk over to your rooms and fetch some of your own clothes for you. Tell me what you need." He waved a hand as if to dismiss my disguise as unthinkable.

I tried to keep my temper. "Creasy, they'll be watching the warehouse. What do you think will happen if they see you walk out of my rooms with a trunk full of ladies apparel? I can't stay here. Dirty or not, those clothes make a good disguise. Now just go and get them." I pointed to the door.

Creasy shrugged. "I can't get them. They're gone." He paused. "I nearly burned them in the back yard, but I put them in the rag bag instead."

"Well, get them out of the ragbag," I ordered.

"I can't. It's been collected. It's probably in the midden by now."

"What?" I rose to my knees, waving my dangling sleeves in furious circles. "What?" The repeated question came out as a shriek.

"Now Hetty...." Creasy took a hasty step backwards.

"Don't you 'Now Hetty' me!" I shouted. "What am I supposed to do? Walk about the streets like this?" I shook my sleeves at him. "Don't you think people will notice? I'm wearing the minister's shirt and little else? That will land me in jail faster than if it'd stayed in Rumney Marsh. What were you thinking, man?" I stopped and concentrated upon taking deep breaths. It wouldn't do to lose control of myself. I had to think. In order to think with clarity, I had to calm myself. No doubt the man meant well...he always did. He'd never seen me in such filthy rags before, after all. (Perhaps thinking with charity would help me to think with clarity.) I took one last deep breath while Creasy stood before me, shifting from one lanky leg to another like a dark stork.

"What are we to do, Creasy?" I looked straight at him, showing command of my temper. "I must leave here and your clothes won't fit me, even if I had the ablest needle in the Bay Colony and time to alter them." Let him come up with a plan; it was his heedless act that put me in this situation.

"Perhaps we can send a boy with a message to your clerk?" Creasy said, voice rising on a note of hope. "I don't have to go near the warehouse that way."

My patience was being sorely tested here. "I don't want my clothes, Creasy. That's the point. If I wear my clothes, I'll be recognized and arrested. I don't want to be arrested. So what if those old rags smelled like dead eels? I like dead eels. You like dead eels… at least you've eaten them when I've stuffed them with spices and boiled them for you. The smell of dead eels kept people away from me. I walked the streets and nobody bothered me. You see? It was an effective disguise." I crossed my arms against my chest, sleeves dangling down.

Creasy's forehead wrinkled in thought. I waited, knowing that thought was foreign to the gentleman. Finally he spoke up, his face lit in expectation.

"I may have a solution, if you not too squeamish about it, Hetty…and I can't think why you would be after wearing those stinking clothes you borrowed. I'm sorry it took so long.… I was trying to recall who took the latest donation of clothing for my congregation. They go out as fast as they come in, you know, the need is so great.… Well, you've been generous with your own donations, of course. Then I remembered that I do have a bundle of women's clothing available. I should have thought of it at once! You should have thought of it, yourself! Arabella Edwards," he burst out. "You left the parcel of her clothing in my care. You can wear them."

After an initial shudder, I agreed. Clothing is passed down in wills as it is a valuable item, so it's not that the woman was dead that gave me pause but the idea of wearing a murdered woman's dress.… Common sense asserted itself. The petticoats are plain and the lady won't be needing them, I reasoned.

"Go get the parcel," I said.

Creasy hastened out the door, returning within minutes with a parcel in his arms.

I took it from him and tore it open. Pulling out the robe, I held it against me.

"Do you have shears or a knife?" I asked, standing up on the bed as I spoke.

Creasy averted his eyes while he fumbled in his coat pocket, producing a small knife.

Without words I pointed to the door. As soon as he left I

jumped down and laid the robe on the bed, pulling the petticoats out to set beside it. I drew Creasy's shirt off and dropped it on the floor. I removed the lacy shift and held it for a moment. The woman who owned this beautiful article enjoyed life. Why would someone take it from her? I shook my head and went about the business of dressing myself in the dead woman's clothing.

Chapter Twenty-two

I glided through the streets of Boston in relative obscurity, keeping away from my usual haunts, my head covered by Arabella's hood. I needed a place to hole up for a few days. As far as the Town magistrates knew, I'd fled in my ship, the *Anhinga*, for unknown waters. That they could tell the Salem sheriff, should he pursue me here. Word of my plight might have all ready arrived, and a warrant for my arrest issued. I needed time to think and for Creasy to make the trip to Rumney Marsh.

The less frequented part of town was the Trimountain—at least respectable people did not frequent it—and my steps led me straight to the home of the Ferret. My little spy would come in handy for errands. As luck would have it, the door burst open as I approached and the Ferret nearly collided with me as he leaped over the doorstep. As it was, a small sibling tripped on Ferret's heels, running smack into my spy's back and falling with a plop onto the ground. The door banged shut to twitterings of laughter. Sharp noses lined the greasy window.

Ferret took a quick step backwards, trodding upon his little brother's worn boot. The boy gave a loud oath. More twitterings came from inside the shack. The youngster sat upon the ground rubbing a thin ankle.

I took a closer look at the boy. "Celia Edwards!" I cried out before I could think. "Where are your nice clothes? What have you done with them?" Honestly, all the money I spent on the child and here she was, as ragged as ever, once more in boy's clothing. At least her face appeared clean.

The child looked up at me with bright blue eyes. "Mrs. Henry? Oh, don't worry. I have all my clothes. Elliphalet lets me wear his when we play here, that's all. So I don't get mine dirty. I'll change back before I go home. Esther would have a mad-fit if I tore my new pinner or dirtied my petticoat." With a sunny smile she jumped to her feet, pushing Ferret aside as if he were no more than dandelion down.

"Elliphalet?" I said, nodding when she pointed to the Ferret.

The young man in question just stood there, staring at me with eyes that were watery blue, like melting ice. He twisted a new knit cap in his paws. He shifted from one foot to another.

"Well, Sir?" I greeted my spy. "Have you no words for me?"

The boy hemmed; Celia gave him a nudge. He shrugged a thin shoulder.

"You look just like her—that dead lady that was murdered! I thought you were a...a ghost, that's what. Give me a start, you did." He jammed the cap upon his head with a defiant stare.

Celia snorted. Before she could tease the boy I felt I should explain.

"These are her clothes that I'm wearing. No wonder you thought you saw a ghost! How clever of you to notice."

Celia's face lit at my announcement. She reached out to touch the striped cloth of the robe.

"These are my mother's clothes?"

"Yes," I said. "You may have them when I'm finished with them. I need them for a disguise." Two small heads nodded, unquestioning. "But surely she has robes and petticoats like this at home?" I asked.

"Oh, her clothes are all wrapped and put away. I made Esther show me one or two gowns but she didn't want me to unwrap them and take them out. It's not the same as seeing you wear them." The child took a fold of the linen gown in her small fingers and caressed it. "I don't remember her much, you see. When I try, her face fades away from me."

Ferret turned to Celia. "Well, I would've thought she was your mother. Now you know what she looked like. You can think of her any time you want." He spoke in a matter of fact voice that the child seemed to accept as good advice. She nodded her agreement, releasing the striped cloth from her fingers.

An idea began to germinate in my mind like dandelion fluff landing upon a pile of dirt. It needed time to take root, but once it's tiny hooks grasped hold it wouldn't budge.

"Celia, does Esther Thripenny still go to bed early and bolt her door?"

Celia nodded. "I pretend to go to bed, too, just so she won't worry about me."

I forbore to ask her what she did after dusk. Some things it is best not to know.

"I'll come over tonight, after she's in bed. You come too, Ferret...we'll use your spy name because I have some spy work for you," I added. "Time for my spies to earn their pay."

Ferret rubbed his hands together in eager anticipation of coin.

Later that evening, the door to Arabella Edward's house was opened to me by her daughter. But not before an owl's hoot alerted her to my arrival. This was a prearranged signal, I'd been told. Ferret would stand guard by hiding in the shrubbery. A similar hoot would warn of intruders during my stay.

Entering as quietly as I could, I glanced around the hallway for signs of the housekeeper.

"Don't worry, Esther's hard of hearing anyway." Celia spoke in a normal tone. "She's in bed, asleep and snoring...if you listen hard you can hear her buzz."

I listened but could not make out any sounds. "What about Joseph? Does he know I'm coming?" I had a particular worry that I might scare the young man as I'd startled Ferret earlier; that he might think me the ghost of Arabella Edwards. Celia informed me that Joseph no longer slept in the kitchen. Esther Thripenny had ordered him home to his own bed.

"I told him it was all right," Celia said. "He's happier sleeping in his own bed, anyway. Esther's mean to him. Besides, our comings and goings would just upset him at night. Joseph likes things to be the same; you go to bed by dark and you get up when it's light outside. That's what he understands."

I thought to myself that perhaps the young man might object to Celia's nighttime forays, so she was just as happy to have him out of the way. I also wondered whether Esther Thripenny was too old to be caretaker of this wily child. Since the only alternative might be for me to take over the task, I could only hope that the child's London aunt would indeed come to New England to live. I asked Celia whether she had thought more upon the subject and was glad to hear that Mister Hacker had written to the aunt on Celia's behalf. Mister Hacker would make all the arrangements necessary; so he'd promised the child. I devoutly hoped that Mister Hacker could be trusted in this respect.

Celia led me into the kitchen, where she seated me upon the table bench and played the proper hostess by offering me a glass of buttermilk. I accepted. She stood beside me, fidgeting from one foot to another, as I drank the cool offering.

"Mister Hacker took away the coins beneath the bed?" I asked. She nodded with vigor.

"He gave you a receipt for them?" I asked.

She gave a little hop, her golden hair flying about her shoulders. "Yes, he did, and I hid it like you said. I told you I could find good hiding places...well, so could my mother. I found something she hid and I want you to see it." She leaned forward over my chair, an eager expression upon her little face.

"I would like to see it," I said, meaning every word.

The child ran off. What had the little imp unearthed? Why hadn't the unknown intruder found it first? He'd ignored a pot of gold beneath the bed; what was it he needed to find? I hardly dared hope it was the answer to Arabella Edward's murder, yet I could feel my innards tingle. I made myself concentrate upon the milk glass in my hand.

Celia returned not two minutes later, although it felt like an hour. She held out a small leather book. "Here. I found this in a little shelf beneath the com...commode chair. That is what Esther said I must call it. Mama was smart. No one would ever think to look for it beneath the chamber pot, would they? And I only found it because I've never seen a com...commode chair before. I wanted to see how it worked. Mama must be very rich to own such a chair! Imagine, being able to shit and piss in a chair!" She shook her tumbled curls in wonder at such luxury.

So should I have had just such a reaction when I was Celia's age. I did not comment and accepted the leather book which she thrust into my hands.

"Bring me a candle, please," I requested in as calm a tone as I could muster. My innards were quaking at this point. The hearthfire was banked for the evening and light was fading from the room.

Celia obliged me before seating herself at my side. As I opened the book to pages of numbers, the child leaned beside me, pointing to the figures. "I am quite good at numbers. I can add them up...Aunt says I have a special talent for it. She can't add numbers or read, either. I can't read yet. Esther is teaching me my letters, though."

I muffled an exclamation of horror. Imagine a child of her age not knowing her letters! Poor imp! Find me a Puritan child who can't read her Bible and I'll show you a blind youngster. (One who probably knows her Bible by heart, nonetheless.)

I forced myself to concentrate upon the small leather volume in my hand and nearly fell off the bench when the figures penetrated my numbed brain.

"Is it an accounts book?" Celia swung her small legs back

and forth in her chair.

"Sort of an accounts book," I answered slowly. "Now hush, Child, while I concentrate."

In a neat hand were recorded payments for secret sins from gambling to bribery paid for government contracts under the former Royal Governor. I could only surmise that the Governor's Secretary of the Provinces, the detested Edward Ruckenmaul, had passed on this information to his mistress before he was shipped away in chains to London. In effect he had insured a steady income to Arabella Edwards. For the last three years certain merchants of Boston had paid well for her silence. No wonder the lady had a cash box full of coins beneath her bed. Should the information become public it would spell ruin for the gentlemen. Not only would they face the magistrates in court, they would be shunned by all good men of commerce in the Colony as traitors. The former Royal Governor Andros was as hated today as he'd been while in office.

I could guess at some of the identities: *The Angel Gabriel* paid a bribe for the privilege of providing His Majesty's Provincial Troops with spirits; a lucrative contract. (My own sources had informed me that M'sieur Germaine smuggled in wines from France, the same country he'd fled.)

The Bookworm—that must be Phillip Boynton—provided special religious materials to the Royal Governor and to his staff. Did booksellers need a special license or stamp? I didn't understand. The Reformed Church did not approve of the Church of England Book of Common Prayer, but there were no rules against it as far as I knew. Nor were there laws against hymnals of another faith. The Huguenots used one with the psalms of Marot—quite lovely, really.

Could it be that Edmund Andros was secretly a Papist and needed special papist prayer materials that Boynton provided? That would be a disastrous revelation in Puritan country. The Royal governor had been accused of collaboration with the Canadian priests, who sent the Indians down upon us. Too many towns on the northern frontiers had been attacked, too many bloody massacres the result.   Perhaps Boynton had some knowledge of this.   If so, and word got out, the man's life was forfeit.   The savage attacks upon our far towns affected us all as refugees poured in with their horrifying tales.   Even we in Boston could not feel secure.   When people do not feel secure in their homes they often bend the law to destructive purposes. I shook my head.   I'd been taught by the late Mr. Henry to always seek justice in the law.

"What's the matter, Hetty?"   Celia stopped her leg-swinging and regarded me.

"It's a matter of doing the right thing, Celia," I answered. "Some people have done naughty things that they try to keep secret.   Your mother wrote about those things in this book."   I leaned towards the child.   "There can be no secrets from God, Child.   Remember that."   Let that be a lesson learned from the follies of others.   I returned to the journal.

There were other names in code that I could not at the moment decipher.   Still, the amounts recorded here did not seem so very outrageous—enough to keep the woman comfortable, but hardly worth murder.   Perhaps someone felt differently.   Perhaps he sought to keep his good name untarnished.   I thumbed through some more pages.   Here was a gambling debt deeded over from Edward Ruckenmaul to A. Edwards for payment, for a considerable sum owed by *Badbones*.   I conjectured this gentleman was the discrete doctor, Geoffrey Malbone, but the amount was steadily paid down to a comfortable level.   I wondered at the folly of mankind. Gambling was a ruinous vice, yet there were worse failings, I knew.   Three pages further and I found the worse.

"What do these letters spell out?"   Celia pointed her small finger at a bold heading.   "That's an A and that's a D and that's a U and an L....   What does it mean?"

"Child, it's not necessary for you to wait here beside me all this time.   Why don't you go out and watch with Fer...Eliphalet?"

"Oh, he'll hoot when anyone comes.   It's our signal.   He

hoots like a real owl." Celia caught up a golden ringlet and twisted it around her finger.

"Well, why don't you have another glass of buttermilk?" I suggested, sliding her empty glass towards her hand. "And have some of those ginger cakes Esther made. I can smell them from here. Leave me be for awhile." I waited until she slid from her seat before I returned to my perusals.

Adulteries and Perversities—that was the heading on a column that ran on for three sheets of fine script. Here I came across the name I'd assumed would fill the book. *H. K'gly's* identity was barely hidden. He made no payments to Arabella for his Adulteries and Perversities, however. It seemed that <u>Mrs.</u> *Beaver, Mistress Fishwife* and *The Thorne* paid dearly for the privilege of sharing a bed with Harry Kegleigh. ("Services offered free," was noted in the margins next to *H. K'gly*.) The unfortunate ladies, however, gave Arabella Edwards twenty pounds a month to keep their trysts secret. Now how did Bella Edwards know about these trysts? Kegleigh, that great ape, had opened his big mouth to brag about his conquests. I had no doubt upon that score.

I wondered who was <u>Master Biggins</u>, the gentleman who liked to be spanked for his naughty behavior and punished by being shut up in a cupboard. Biggins is a child's cap, not the name of anyone I knew in Town. Nor did I recognize any seaman by the name of *Captain Bluebeard* who would consent to being manacled and whipped and pay for the privilege. The captains I knew gave out that punishment to unruly crewmen. Some captains enjoyed carrying out the sentence themselves, to be sure, but I could not imagine a one of them opting to receive a dozen lashes.

I was almost certain *The Bull* was code for Kegleigh, whose perversities included abduction and the use of force. "Prefers the lady to struggle," was noted in neat letters by the name. Kegleigh said he never paid Bella Edwards for her body but the man split hairs. *The Bull* presented his lady-love with gifts that were neatly recorded: "amber beads," which were then sold for ten pounds; "pearl earrings" went for twelve; "kid gloves with lace cuffs" went for five, and so on for a full column. So much for Kegleigh's tokens of affection. I wondered if he knew how the lady benefited from his generosity or if he would care. Could he have discovered the venal manner in which she'd treated his gifts and in a moment of rage strung up the lady?

And who was Long Sally, who took a dish of tea with Arabella on Monday afternoons? What was perverse about taking tea? Turning the page I understood why taking tea with Arabella Edwards became a costly endeavor. Long Sally not only paid for the privilege of Arabella's company, there was the additional cost for gold braided gowns and embroidered petticoats for Long Sally to wear, all in the latest London fashion. Not to mention the costly black lace that lined the undergarments. "I begged the black lace shift of him but he would not part with it," Arabella noted in her round hand. "He promised me one made in my own fit." I couldn't help wondering if I could find the gift in her chest of clothes.

"What are you reading about now?" Celia stood beside me, munching upon a slice of ginger cake.

"Fashions, Celia," I spoke hurriedly. "Your mother writes of fashions." How could I explain it to her otherwise?

"My mother wore very fine clothes," the child said.

"Yes, she did. And you shall wear them some day." I smiled at the child but my hand nudged her away with a firm touch. "Now run along and see if Eliphalet is lonesome. You can both guard the house for me so no one finds me here. Hide in the bushes or something."

"We'll hoot if anybody comes," she assured me, taking her leave with a cheerful wave.

I confess I was anxious to see what other details were recorded in the book. I noted that Arabella made interesting little sketches of ruching and braiding and patterns of embroidery found on the clothing Long Sally wore in her company. If only I could discover the identity of this gentleman, I would be sure to ask for the address of his seamstress.

I sincerely hoped no one came while I examined this journal. I couldn't afford to be found here, in the dead woman's house. Nor did I want to confront the murderer by myself. I had arrangements to make before that happened. Details of a plan were swirling around in my head; I needed time to put them in order.

I skimmed over several more pages to the final two sheets, which were listings of trinkets with no names attached. Here were objects of under five pounds-worth in value but dutifully recorded by the good businesswoman that was Arabella Edwards: gloves, ribbons, combs, hair ornaments. I closed the book with a sigh. Where was Froggy? Which one was he? Why wasn't the name recorded in this volume? Could there be another volume somewhere? The book's last listing was dated a week prior to her death.

I wished Creasy were back so that he could help me sort through the tangle of suspects this slender volume presented. There were almost too many to handle.

Best to start with the ones we knew, I told myself, and gave my thoughts to forming my plan.

Chapter Twenty-three

The notes were sent out but not before a balk from the Ferret, who stood before me scuffing a bare toe in the dirt. It turned out that young Elliphalet had never set dirty foot off the Trimountain in his short life. The thought of venturing into unfamiliar territory unnerved the young gentleman. His eye brightened at the offer of extra coin then quickly dimmed as he shook his head. Celia saved the day by taking his hand in her own, peering beneath his cap and assuring him that she would go with him.

"I knew some of the streets here and I would like to see more of this town. You have no idea how many people live in London, 'Phalet. Why, there are so many people on the streets, so many carts and horses and coaches and chairs that carry people.... Why it is almost impossible to move about! And you would have to cover your ears at the noise. You would have to cover your ears, believe me, 'Phalet." Her little head bobbed up and down with vigor. "Boston is a small town, really. It won't be hard to find our way at all. Don't be frightened."

Ferret pulled away from her, a thin lower lip thrust out. "Feered is it? I ain't feered. I just don't know the way is all."

"Mrs. Henry will tell us." Celia looked over at me, her face beaming good will.

"I'll draw you a map," I offered. I wasn't sure that Ferret could read.

So I made my plans: two strong villains for protection, summons sent for Gabriel Germaine, Phillip Boynton and Harry Kegleigh to appear at the home of the late Arabella Edwards at the hours of nine, ten and eleven o'clock respectively. It was a start.

I eliminated Oliver Hacker from these suspects. As Edward Ruckenmaul's clerk and Arabella Edward's man of business, he must have passed on information to her. He would have no reason to kill his partner in whatever schemes had been hatched between them to make profitable use of the information. So long as he did well by Bella's daughter he need fear no hindrance from me. We all have our little secrets in trade that are best kept in the shadows.

I'd stayed well away from my rooms above the warehouse, fearing that they were watched, but I'd had Celia carry a note to my clerk's wife. Betsy brought her husband's dinner to the warehouse every day. This day she walked away with a bundle of my clothing hidden in the dinner basket. Celia and Ferret carried the bundle to me. The two were turning out to be very helpful little spies. Celia was quick witted and bright beyond her years.

Ferret did not learn quite as fast but once his initial reluctance to go into town was overcome, he proved himself resourceful and determined. When he learned a route to a particular house, he also scouted alleys and byways that offered quick means of escape. Celia said he'd begun to take the lead in their forays.

Celia helped me find the appropriate dress for my performance. The striped gown I'd worn had begun to smell as if it came from the grave, which might make it appropriate, but I wished for something more of a spectral nature. And I was sick of wearing the same gown. Celia thought she'd seen a white gown in the chest so we rummaged through Arabella's clothing – carefully rummaged—until we unearthed a white lustring dress shot through with silver threads. Wrapped in the same parcel was a white linen petticoat with a wide border of silver. Just the thing for moonlight haunting, I judged. The seams showed wear, the hem was slightly stained. That meant that Arabella had worn the gown more than once, so it was likely the gentlemen had seen her in the apparel and would perhaps recognize it as hers.

"What shall I wear on my head?" I spoke aloud. "I should cover my head." Arabella's gold locks were her outstanding feature, as I understood it. My own locks were blond, but of a dark honey hue.

"She's got lacy things in the chest of drawers." Celia jumped up from fingering a plum velvet gown and ran to a tall chest of cherry wood.

I remained upon my knees and carefully replaced the paper of the parcels we'd opened so that Esther Thripenny could not blame the little girl for disturbing the carefully packed clothing.

"Look! Look!" Celia called to me. She held a mantle of lace spread out across her arms.

"Oh, my!" I closed the lid and rose to my feet. Upon inspection the Flemish lace was as gossamer as a spider's web. I couldn't repress a twinge of envy. The lady had excellent connections in the London trade – the Protestant Belgian lace makers had fled to London from the persecutions of King Louis of France—but then I'd known about her connections.

"Here…use this as a veil." Celia threw a cloud of lace over my head, where it floated light as mist. "Let your hair down loose. The veil will cover it and your face…." She stood back to examine the effect. "You'll look like a proper ghost in that," she nodded, satisfied.

I sincerely hoped the child was right. My plan was to confront my suspects with the ghostly apparition of Arabella Edwards. As soon as they stepped through the gate I would materialize from behind a lilac bush and walk along the hedge towards my quarry, then I'd slip through a break in the hedge and disappear from sight.

Celia and I went outside for a trial walk, the veil over my head, but the Ferret declared from the gate that he couldn't see me for beans. I'd have to make a scary noise to announce my presence. He and Celia began to moan and growl as examples of what I could do to attract attention. Since the object was for me to be seen, not heard, I came up with a plan to place lanterns behind the hedge. The lanterns would be lit but covered with a dark cloth. Ferret would remove the dark cloths as I walked on the other side of the hedge and Celia would follow him with a candlesnuffer, putting out each light as I passed. This worked to perfection; a spectral glow lit my figure in as an unearthly a sight as would frighten the Devil into confessing his sins, or so the two children declared. They were both pleased to take part in the performance, which I had first forbidden as dangerous. Ferret even added a nice touch by fashioning a noose to wear about my neck. He adjusted the knot so that I wouldn't choke in case I stumbled or met with some other accident. He also powdered the rope in keeping with my ghastly appearance.

My bullyboys would be stationed by the gate and by the break in the hedge. They had their orders to protect me from attack and to protect the children, if necessary. They would also serve as witnesses to a confession of murder. I did indeed think I could frighten a confession from the villain—who wouldn't confess when confronted by a ghostly apparition? He wouldn't know that he was being observed—any confession he made was to the grave. I thought my friend Creasy would approve of my plan. He'd make an excellent witness if he were here. On the other hand, he'd probably object that I was putting myself in the way of danger. He might even suggest that he dress up as Arabella's ghost, which would not do. A tall, gawky ghost wouldn't fool anyone. Either that, or he'd insist upon protecting me himself. While I knew Creasy wasn't afraid of a fight, I had more faith in my two bullyboys and their big cudgels. Perhaps it was best that he remained in Salem.

As the time for our first guest approached I felt confident that all contingencies were considered. My two burly ruffians had their instructions: to capture and bind the murderer and to deliver him to the magistrates; to let the others run away at will. (I couldn't see them sticking around once they'd seen Arabella's ghost.) Above all, the bullies were to protect me and the children. The lanterns were lit; everyone assumed their places. I took my station behind the lilac bush on the right side of the house, the children behind the hedges, the bullyboys at their places, thick cudgels ready.

I didn't need Ferret's owl hoot to realize that M'sieur Germaine had arrived; he came rattling up in his coach with horses stomping, bells jingling, whips cracking and French curses bawled out at the top of the coachman's lungs. M'sieur made enough noise to wake the dead. Which he must have thought was the case as he stepped through the creaking gate.

I materialized and floated toward him in a ghostly glow. To add to the effect I shook the rope around my neck before raising my arm and thrusting an accusing finger at him. I groaned. I couldn't help myself, the groan just slipped out. At the break in the hedge I slipped through, disappearing from his sight. A huge black shape stood by my side; my bullyboy at the ready. His presence was a comfort to me, for I didn't know how Germaine would react. I stooped beside the hedge and peered through the bottom branches, hoping to witness a confession.

At first I couldn't see anything, but I heard a loud cry, an answering shout and the footman came running with a lantern in his hand. I saw M'sieur upon his knees, one hand clutching his chest, the other raised as if to ward off the Devil. He cried out in disjointed gasps.

"Lord...angels...have mercy! Have mercy upon me! Oh, poor dead creature...why do you haunt me? Why do you torment me? I never harmed you...Christ be my witness...." The gentleman then fell to the ground, writhing and sobbing with a force that shook his body. The coachman leaned over him, set the lantern upon the grass and attempted to comfort him.

Disjointed phrases came to my ears: "Wouldn't harm... poor lady...breaks my heart...angels...mercy...oh, my heart!"

The coachman finally succeeded in raising his master from

the ground. M'sieur Germaine, sobs still shaking his body, leaned heavily upon the man as he was led back through the gate to the coach. In short order we heard the whip crack, the coach creak as it turned, the horses neigh, more French curses and the stomp of hooves as the coach pulled away.

We came out from our respective places behind the hedge.

"He's not the one we're after," I said, trying to keep my voice steady. The poor man's display of fright and grief affected me deeply. What agony had I put him through? I expected to frighten my subjects but I hadn't meant to cause them palpitations of the heart! What if the gentleman had died of fright? I would be as much a murderer as the killer of Arabella Edwards, whom I sought to uncover. I found I was trembling.

The two ruffians stood silent, smacking their cudgels against their hands. If they were disappointed at losing their quarry, they hid it behind stolid exteriors.

Celia and Ferret did nothing to hide their jubilation: "We did it! We did it!" The two jumped up and down, giggling.

"Fraidy cat! Fraidy cat! Did you see how scared he was? Did you hear him cry? What a big fat fraidy cat!" Celia shouted.

"Children." I held out my hand in warning. "Celia, you must not mock the gentleman. He had reason to be frightened. Wouldn't you be frightened if you saw a ghost?"

Celia grabbed my gown and pulled upon it. "You were a wonderful ghost, Hetty! Just like a real ghost. You really scared him, and the lights worked just like we planned! Oh, isn't this the best trick ever?"

I caught at the child's hand, prying open her fingers to release my gown. "Celia, we are not here to play tricks on honest citizens, we are here to catch the man who murdered your mother. You must remember that."

My stern warning did little to curb the child's enthusiasm. "You did make a good ghost," she called out as she bounced away with Ferret to hide behind the hedge. I could hear their giggles.

"Light the lanterns again," I ordered.

Turning to the two bullyboys, I addressed them in a lowered tone. "Gentlemen, I must warn you that the other two men I expect to come here will probably act in a vastly different manner. There may even be violence. Be vigilant." I thought of Harry Kegleigh, the great ape. I didn't want my fellows to let down their guard after seeing M'sieur Germaine's display. I needn't have worried.

"We're ready," said my bodyguard of the hedge. He spoke in a raspy voice. The big wooden club in his hand he lifted in reassurance.

I nodded. We drifted apart to take our stations for the next visitor. Celia and the Ferret whispered together as they lit and covered each lantern behind the hedge. I heard their stifled giggles.

Conscience bid me confess that I had enjoyed myself while acting out this role. I felt I was a credible specter as I glided along the hedge. Pride, that damnable vanity, is my besetting sin. Still, I must keep up my performance to serve a greater good. While the belief in spirits and ghosts is universal, I was certain that Boynton's and Kegleigh's reactions would not be as dramatic as that of poor M'sieur Germaine. I cold not help feeling guilt over that poor gentleman. I hadn't meant to frighten anyone to death, which I'd nearly done. As I waited for Boynton's arrival at my station behind the bush, I wondered if I was any different from those young women in Salem Town. Their silly tales of spirits pinching and biting were the cause of one death and many jailings of good people. Not all of the accused were witches, as I had cause to know. I consoled myself with the knowledge that my aim in playing this prank was to unmask a murderer. With that thought I must be content.

Time seemed to drag its feet. Perhaps Boynton would not come? I half hoped he would not. I adjusted my skirts and shifted the noose around my neck to show to best advantage. When the owl hoot came, I took a deep breath.

When I heard the creak of the gate I stepped from my hiding spot and glided before the hedge in a mist of light. At the opening I paused, lifting my hand in languid movement as if it took some effort to do so. I pointed the finger of accusation.

I was correct in my estimation that Phillip Boynton would not react in quite the same manner as had poor M'sieur. This gentler man stood with knees slightly bent, legs apart, feet firmly planted in a defensive posture. His hand reached to his hip. I glimpsed a flash of silver as Boynton pulled out his sword. Light glinted off the sharp tip of steel as it circled in the air, much like a hound sniffing out its quarry. I froze like a rabbit, afraid to move, my eyes fixed upon that cruel tip. My mind triumphed that here indeed we had found our murderer! My body, however, warned that I could well be the next victim. And the light continued to shine behind me, making me a fine target.

"Put out the light! Put out the light!" My frantic appeal was whispered from the side of my mouth, directed to the other side of the hedge.

Blessed darkness descended as I slid through the hedge. I heard a loud smack and a cry over the pounding of my heart as I sank to the grass. Through the brush I saw lights flaring upon the lawn. My guardian bounded past me, terse commands rang in the air and a little hand pulled upon my gown. I reminded myself to breathe again.

"Did you see that?" A dirty little imp materialized howling at my elbow. Was I back in Salem at the courthouse? Did my mind play tricks upon me? The imp hopped up and down in continuous motion.

"Did you see that? Smash! He went down like an ox. One hit! Maybe he's dead. C'mon, let's go see!" And the imp hopped away. The tugging upon my dress continued. Were there two imps? Was I plagued by imps sent by the Prince of Darkness to torment me? Listen, I told myself, the thing addresses me.

"Hetty...Hetty...I had trouble with the last light. It

wouldn't go out. Sorry! You looked like a real ghost, though, just standing there all in white...."

Had the gentleman run me through with his sword, I would have been a real ghost, I thought, unable as yet to work my tongue. Wordless, I rose from the safety of the grass and followed the tug upon my gown as Celia pulled me back through the hedge. There a tableau of deviltry made me shudder. Flames from a torch revealed two dark figures bent over a prone body while an imp of Satan danced about the trio in high glee. Oh, hellish vision!

"Is he dead?" I hurried forward. How would I ever explain this to the magistrates? Even a murderer must have his day in court, or so my late husband believed. Mr. Henry would be sorely disappointed in me if I'd usurped the court's rights.

My two ruffians straightened. One turned to address me. "Not dead. He'll wake up with a sore head, is all. I coshed him a good one. What do you want us to do with him?" The voice held a gruff but hopeful note, as if I should allow them to dispose of the body in the nearest swamp.

Chapter Twenty-four

My hand upon the gentleman's waistcoat above his heart reassured me of his life. "Carry him into the house," I directed my two ruffians.

One man lifted his legs, the other lifted poor Mr. Boynton under the arms and the gentleman was transported into the kitchen. He was deposited upon the high-backed settle before the hearth, his head lolling against the curve of the wooden arm.

"Get a pillow," I said to Celia. "And there's a bottle of yellow liquid on a stand in the parlor...bring that, too." As the child ran to do my bidding I turned to the two men. "Build up the fire and there's a tumbler of brandy for you each. You, Fer...Eliphalet. Get me a bucket of water, if you please." Let the imp put his energy to good use.

I excused myself and hurried to Celia's bedroom where I pulled the noose from my neck and slipped out of the silver gown, replacing it with my own plain linen dress and apron. I ran back to the kitchen where I found clean cloths in the ragbag. With my bullyboy's help, I straightened the poor gentleman upon the settle and examined his injury. Dipping a cloth in cool water, a careful wash revealed nothing worse than a big goose egg rising upon the back of the gentleman's head. A cool compress would take care of that.

At my ministrations, the gentleman groaned. One eye opened. I waved the two ruffians into the background while I addressed the injured man, bending over him. "I've a pillow here. Can you lift your head?"

The gentleman moaned, opened his other eye and attempted to comply with my request. I took the pillow from Celia's hands and slipped it behind his head. "Drink this, you'll feel better for it." I held a small thimble glass of brandy to his lips.

Boynton sucked it down, smacking his lips like a babe in arms. I had Celia refill the glass.

"Slowly," I cautioned as Boynton coughed and groaned at the same time. Liquid dribbled from his lips. His eyes seemed to be looking at each other. I motioned for Celia to hold up a candle, the better to inspect him as he drank. Color seeped back into his face, which had looked as white as the underbelly of a fish. I was much encouraged to see it.

"Can you talk?" I spoke in a gentle tone, believing I had the advantage of the gentleman, who was in a weakened state. A show of sympathy often opens a man's mouth.

"What happened?" The gentleman raised his hand to his head, wincing as he felt the bandage there. "Am I dead?" Bewilderment turned to panic as the hearth fire chose that moment to burst into brilliant flames. "Oh my good Lord," he gasped. "Oh Lord, forgive...."

"No, no, you're not dead, not at all. That's only the hearth fire," I soothed. "You are in the house of Arabella Edwards."

"Arabella...." He raised his hand to his head, exploring the compress there with cautious fingers. For a brief moment his eyes lost their focus. "Ouch! My head hurts."

"You've had a nasty bump, that's all," I said, my tone reassuring.

"How...?" He regarded me with the trusting look of a child.

"You drew your sword," I said.

"I did?" The man's brows rose in bewilderment.

"You did. Why did you draw your sword?" I asked.

The gentleman shook his head, promptly wincing at the

pain.

"Don't remember," he mumbled.

"Do you remember anything?" I kept my voice sympathetic. I catechized him on his identity, his address, my identity – he paused but identified me correctly—and did he remember Arabella Edwards?

"Of course," he huffed, his brows settled into a frown.

"Why did you murder Arabella Edwards?" I threw the question at him, hoping to shock the truth from him.

"Why would I murder Arabella Edwards?" His eyes grew wide in amazement.

"Did she blackmail you?"

"Why would she blackmail me?"

Perhaps his puzzlement was genuine, I thought, considering that he had a large bump upon his head. I prompted him to remember.

"Your books?" I wasn't certain what the books would have to do with blackmail, but she listed payments for books under his name.

"My books? What of my books?"

"We know you made payments to her for the books."

"Of course I paid her for her work on the books. She's quite...was quite expressive with her illustrations," he amended, with an awkward pause. "My readers want to see her work. I shall have problems finding another artist with her talent, I assure you." He groaned and touched his compress. "My poor head!"

I offered the gentleman another thimble of brandy. As he drank, I whispered an aside to Celia to make up Joseph's fireside cot for another occupant. Boynton would never make it back to town in his current condition.

"So you paid her for her portraits? Like a limner?" I was amazed, my voice rising to a squeak.

"If you will...I prefer to think of her more as an artist of landscapes. Her work is...was...exquisite." His eyes took on a misty daze. "She knew how her work would translate to print. That's rare. Well, I found her in a printing shop in London, you know. Bella had a good back ground in how the presses work…invaluable to me."

"So you had no reason to do away with her?" I spoke my thought aloud.

"No reason whatsoever, I assure you, Madame!" Boynton regarded me with rounded eyes, as if I were a madwoman who must be mollified. "I paid her well for her work," he continued. "My books are classics of the Far East, you know. Bella has…had a true artist's appreciation for the stories. Errr," he paused a fraction, adjusting the froth of lace that fell from his throat. "If these stories might seem a bit lascivious to our modern tastes, the fact remains that they are regarded as classic tales in their own cultures. Many people appreciate them, even some of your own Reformed Church people, I might add. Of course I cannot reveal the identity of my clients—that would never do."

"You mean Arabella Edwards…she painted pictures for these books?" I seemed to be particularly dense in understanding this evening. Perhaps it was the night air.

"Sketches in ink, to be precise. Which were then transferred onto blocks for printing. She knew the process, as I say."

"You say you met her in a printer's shop?" I asked.

"In London," he nodded, and immediately groaned, raising his hand to the compress upon his head. "She was too beautiful and too lively to bury herself in a printer's shop. I offered her an escape from that life."

"As an artist to illustrate your books?" I asked.

"As my mistress." A note of impatience crept into his voice. "Lord, but she was a lovely creature—like a newly minted gold coin." His eyes misted over; for a moment he was lost to me.

"Oh," I said. "But she was with Secretary Ruckenmaul here in Boston. Were you angry with her for leaving you?" Boynton might still have a motive for her killing. Jealousy is as old as the hills.

The gentleman snorted. "Who do you think introduced them? It was the making of us both. Edward Ruckenmaul gave me access to a rich market for my books and Bella gained entrance to the highest society, a feat beyond her wildest dreams. Oh, she always kept a kind of loyalty to me—she continued to sketch for my books, even as she willingly followed Edward to this wilderness. With Edward's unforeseen return to London...." He paused, clearing his throat as he measured me.

Edward Ruckenmaul had been sent back in chains by our people to be tried on charges of graft and corruption. I certainly applauded that triumph of ours.

"Truth be told, I think she was glad to have my work," he added, "and I was certainly glad to have her talents. You have no idea how successful my venture has become, even here in Boston. Yes, this is a place where people appreciate books. Of course, I still have my London clients."

"London...? Why did you choose to settle here? I would think your...readers would be in greater number there." I felt curious now about this successful chapman. What kind of books did he purvey?

"Ahhh...." Boynton rubbed his head, avoiding the compress as he did so. "It became a delicate matter...one of Bella's illustrations came too close to the mark, I'm afraid. What makes her work so successful, besides her delicate lines, is a certain playful satire that our readers seem to enjoy. Well, you know that satire is all the rage in literature nowadays."

"Oh, satire," I said, relieved. If that was all the books were about I could see no objection. Satire was quite respectable.

"Yes. A certain member of the royal family didn't like being satirized. Bella was in Boston when the book came out. I thought it prudent to follow her." Boynton fumbled in his coat pocket. "Here, I'll just show you a sample of her work." He pulled out a book the size of a hymnal. "Look at the clear lines, the delicate hand, the light and playful quality. I'll never find another to replace her. Never." Boynton sighed. He set the book upon his knee and opened it for my inspection.

I gazed at an engraving of a woman upon a swing. The woman was almond-eyed, with long dark hair flowing around her body, which was very lightly clad in a scarf of some sort. The woman possessed a well-formed bosom, which was being eyed with appreciation by a turbaned gentleman with large mustachios. The gentleman wore a gauzy gold vest over a bare and muscular chest—you could see droplets of sweat glistening there—and light trousers of the same material. The oriental gentleman held a staff of wood in his hands. Upon closer inspection I realized my mistake and blushed, thinking of a certain Mohawk of my acquaintance.

Boynton, seeing my blush, apologized. "But I assure you, I have many fine ladies as customers," he added, "some of the highest society. Now what I wish you to examine is the element of satire here. Do you see the face peering out from behind the shrubbery?" He pointed out the spot with a finger; the nail was clean and trimmed.

With his guidance, I made out two beetled brows, a hawk nose and a sensuous mouth. The face was leering at the playful couple in the center of the illustration. "Secretary Ruckenmaul?" I could not help a cry of surprise. "But...wasn't he angry at her for this?"

"On the contrary," Boynton beamed. "Her subjects were flattered to appear in her work. Look." He pointed to swirling clouds in the sky. With a quick motion he outlined a curling periwig, two eyes, a long mustache and a thin-lipped but smiling mouth, which seemed to bless the two lovers below.

"The Royal Governor?" I squealed.

"The Royal Governor, Edmund Andros himself. And see those hills in the background?" Once more his finger moved, circling, revealing a couple locked in fornication. "You can just make out a birthmark on the lady's thigh...."

"I see," I said, nodding.

"The lady recognized herself by it and was quite delighted. Of course she was equally delighted that you can't make out the identity of her lover. Bella knew when to be discrete, as a rule.

Ah, such talent! I cannot believe she's gone. Such a loss. Such a loss."

I thought his regret sincere, so I allowed him his moment of reflection. I watched as Celia placed a pillow and a blanket neatly upon the cot by the hearth until Boynton claimed my attention.

"Bella promised me a new sketch for the next book. Indeed, she told me it was almost done. Esther Thripenny looked for it among her papers but could not find it. She promised to inform me just as soon as it comes to light. It will be her last...I shall make the book a kind of memorial to her." Boynton leaned back upon the settle, closing his eyes with a grunt.

I suggested that he lie down upon the cot and rest. "Just for an hour or so, Sir. It will do you good.

"No... no.... I should be on my way."

He looked with longing at the cot. I held out my hand to him. "Nonsense. You've had a nasty blow to the head." I spoke with firmness.

He let me pull him upright. "Yes. How did I get the blow, anyhow?"

"You must not leave now," I said, ignoring his question. "You might fall off your horse and do yourself a real injury. I promise to look in upon you in an hour, Sir. Then you may feel up to riding down the Trimountain." I led him over to the cot. He did not protest. I was most anxious to move on to my next appointment but I really felt I could not send the gentleman off with a sore head. Especially since it was my fault he had a sore head.

Boynton closed his eyes as soon as he lay down. I tiptoed from the room and made haste to don my ghostly garments. I sped out the front door to my post behind the lilac.

"Celia...Eliphalet...gentlemen...." I hissed into the dark. "Are we all at our places?"

"What took you so long?" Celia whispered to me from behind the hedge. "Is the gentleman safe?"

"He won't bother us," I said.

We waited as Harry Kegleigh's appointment came and went. I heard rustlings in the hedge and was about to step from my place when Ferret's owl hoot sounded. In short order the sounds of deep voices singing and hollering reached my ears. I heard the creak of saddle leather and the uneven rhythm of horses hooves; two animals, I thought, and two men. Curse the scoundrel! He brought reinforcements with him. The singing was slurred; a great deal of commotion, of creaking leather, of guffaws, came to my ears. The two men were dismounting, evidently with some problems. I distinguished Kegleigh's growl. What if he brought more men? Would my own two ruffians be outnumbered? The thought of a brawl upon the front lawn made me uneasy. I had to think of the children's safety.

"Damn near broke my ankle," Kegleigh complained. I heard the creak of the gate and a loud bang.

Kegleigh's companion giggled. "Couldn't walk if you broke your leg, Fool."

"Didn't walk—rode my horse here. See, there he is, over there." Kegleigh's words were slurred. "Tied to the railing, right there. Now who's the fool?"

"You're drunk, Harry."

"So are you, Tom."

"Let's drink to that!"

I stuck my head out from behind the bush. The two men were passing a flask back and forth with noisy slurps and belches. Oh fine, I thought, the two of them are inebriated. At least my crew ought to be able to handle them if there's any trouble. And maybe a drunken Kegleigh would be ripe for a confession after he'd seen the ghost of his victim. With that in mind, I stepped from my bush and glided before the hedge.

"You're going too fast," a child's voice hissed from behind me.

I slowed my pace. Still, I was half way down the hedge before I was even noticed.

"Lookee...lookee, Harry, there's a lady! C'mon, Sweetings,

give us a kiss!" Kegleigh's companion reached out with both arms, stumbling off balance. He landed on one knee, like an ardent suitor. Kegleigh bent over with laughter.

I reached my final light and paused, pointing my finger at the great oaf. I felt no need to moan or make any sound. Meanwhile, Kegleigh's companion kept calling for a kiss. I felt disgusted with the two men; this was not going as planned. They should be frightened by this apparition, not amorous towards it. I reached up with my left hand and shook the noose about my neck. Kegleigh should be reminded of what he'd done.

Kegleigh's companion finally realized what he was seeing; he spoke in a loud whisper: "Not a lady, Harry, it's a ghost. Can't kiss a ghost. Wouldn't feel a thing. Lips would go right through it."

Kegleigh straightened, staring at me. I shook my finger once at him and slipped through the hedge. A large black shape next to me reassured me that my ruffian was alert and ready for trouble. I knelt beside him, peering through the roots of the hedge. Would he confess? I held my breath.

"Where'd it go, Harry? Can't see it anymore." Tom lurched to his feet, grabbing Kegleigh's shoulder to steady himself. "Can't see the ghost."

Kegleigh reached out for his companion as if he, too, needed steadying. "Not a ghost, Tom. Bella...Bella's spirit. Come to haunt me because I wasn't there to protect her."

"Nice lady, Bella," Tom muttered. He took out the flask, raised it to his mouth, lowered it, looked into it, shook it and dropped it on the ground. "Allus good for a laugh and a leg-over."

Kegleigh stared into the darkness. "Don't you worry, Bella!" He called out in a voice loud enough to wake the dead. "I'll avenge you yet! I won't rest 'til I kill the bastard who hung you! I swear, Bella...I swear to it. Dirty bastard...I'll beat him to a pulp for you, Bella."

Tom pulled Kegleigh back. "C'mon, Harry. Let's go. Need a drink...don't like ghosts. Let's go drink to Bella, Harry.

She'd like that. Put her spirit to rest, and all."

"Drink to her." Kegleigh staggered backwards. "Drink a toast to the lady. That's good. Beat the bastard bloody... that's good, too. " He allowed himself to be pulled back through the gate by his companion.

Soon enough I heard the creaking of saddles, a few curses and the clip-clop of hooves. I breathed a sigh of relief. There had been no confession—it seems I was wrong about Kegleigh—but no brawl, either. For the latter I was thankful. Had he not been so drunk we might have had a very rough time indeed. Now I must consider what to do next.

Chapter Twenty-five

I paid my bullyboys and sent them on their way. The two children protested at my suggestion that it was late and their beds awaited them.

"But I'm not sleepy!" Even in the dark I could see Celia's lips form a pout. "I don't want to go to bed."

The Ferret hopped from one foot to the other. "Don't go to bed this early," he declared, disdain in his tone. "Can't. No room in the bed for me. I wait till the twins get up."

"Nonetheless..." I pointed to the gate.

Ferret and Celia exchanged glances. The ferret shrugged a scrawny shoulder and turned to slink down the path. I waited until the gate creaked before I attempted to reason with Celia.

"But I'm not sleepy!" She repeated this for the fourth time. "Wasn't it exciting when that man drew his sword? Weren't you frightened, Hetty? He might have run it right through you, then you would have gushed buckets of blood all over and he would guess that you weren't a real ghost." The bloodthirsty child waved her arms about.

I attempted to dampen her enthusiasm with a stern lecture. "And had I been run through, it might have served me right for my deception. I tell you this because it is not the Lord's will to deceive your fellow man. It is wrong of me to have involved you in our deception...."

"And 'Phalet?" she interrupted. "Because if it was wrong for me, it was wrong to involve 'Phalet, too."

"Yes, I concede your point. It was certainly wrong of me to involve Eliphalet in my plan, but you see, he is in my employ as a spy. That makes it a little different. My deception was wrong of itself, but it serves a greater good. You understand, Celia, that a greater wrong has been done to your mother. In the pursuit of justice for her, I found it necessary to practice a certain amount of deception." I thought the child was about to interrupt me again, so I held up my hand. "We have yet to discover her murderer. He has not come forward to confess his sin. So we are forced into using a ruse...a trick, if you will, to get him to confess."

"But none of those men confessed," she said, "so what was the good?"

"The good is that we have eliminated three men from our inquiries. We now know that neither of those men murdered your mother. Even though we have yet to catch the true villain, we have accomplished something of merit. Now I must go and send Mr. Boynton on his way. It wouldn't do for Mistress Esther to discover a strange man in her kitchen in the morning."

Celia giggled.

"It will be best if you are in bed and asleep when she rises. We don't want poor Esther to spoil our plan for tomorrow night," I hinted. Celia took the bait.

"Tomorrow? Are we going to do this again? Oh, 'Phalet will be excited! I haven't ever played such a fine prank upon anyone in my life! Thank you, thank you, Hetty, for including us. It really is a splendid trick, and as you say, it is for a greater good. It makes me feel so proud that I can help to catch the bad man who hung my mother."

"Yes, well you are going to need a good night's sleep so that you have your wits about you tomorrow evening." I took her by the shoulder and marched her into the house. Celia went with willing steps, chattering all the way, suggesting means to make me look even more ghastly for the next evening.

I threw a cloak over my costume and directed Celia to take

the blanket from the sleeping gentleman and restore it to its rightful place, lest Esther find something amiss. The child tugged with ruthless determination, pulling the blanket from the man's embrace. She ran off with her prize.

I shook the gentleman's shoulder, at first gently, then with firm shoves. Boynton opened his eyes. He appeared groggy but his two eyes were focused upon me.

"How do you feel? Do you feel up to riding home now? You've had a nice rest," I added.

Boynton sat up with some haste. "Where am I?" He looked around the room. Reaching up to touch his head, he winced once, and then regarded me. "Ah...yes, I seem to have bumped my head. I'm much obliged to you, Madam, for your hospitality. I regret the inconvenience...." He heaved himself from the cot. "I shall take my leave now."

I watched him with care, for I could not in conscience send him home upon his horse if he were truly unable to ride. Yet how I would explain him to Esther Thripenny in the morning, I could not imagine. The gentleman stood straight and his steps were steady. I judged him well enough to make the trip, so I led him through the parlor to the front door. He turned with a short wave for me.

As I saw him stride down the path to the gate, a sudden lethargy overtook me. The thought of the empty kitchen cot lured me like a siren. All I wished was to lie upon it and sleep until daybreak. But by that time, Esther would be up to kindle the fire and begin preparations for breakfast. Esther Thripenny must not find me here. She must not sniff even the faintest whiff of my plans. Esther's son was on the list for the next three suspects. With some mental calculations, I'd included Ephrata Phinny, Doctor Malbone and a merchant named Jenkins, whom I suspected might be the *Captain Bluebeard* in the diary. As for Esther's son, he must have met Bella many times at the house. As for a reason to murder the poor woman, perhaps he felt she brought shame upon his mother's name. Perhaps that was why he'd changed his name to Phinny. In any event, I would write out three more notes in the morning.

Right now, I needed a good night's sleep.

Throwing my cloak over my shoulders, I trudged to the gate, felt it creak beneath my hand and set off down the road. I was too tired to consider the evening's events; I could barely manage to place one foot in front of the other. The incline pulled me down the hill, for which I was grateful. All I had to do was to remain upright and let my feet do my thinking. Any more than that was impossible. I'd never felt such exhaustion in my life; I trudged onward. It was almost a mercy when my senses fell into a black void.

I came to consciousness feeling stiff, damp and cold. I had the odd sensation that I wanted to fall forward but could not. Something prevented me. Where was I? My eyes couldn't penetrate the darkness surrounding me. My ears caught the soothing slap of water upon sand. At almost the same moment my nostrils inhaled the stink of rotting fish. Perhaps I'd tripped and fallen down near the old shack I used as a temporary refuge? It was close by the harbor. If I'd fallen, I must make the effort to get up. Warmth and a dry bed must surely be a few yards away.

I tried to raise my arms but could not move them. I had better luck with my feet, which moved from side to side at my command. When I tried to draw them in under me, I became aware of a hard substance pressing into my back. Once more I felt the sensation that I ought to fall forward and this thing prevented me.

"The Devil?" I muttered.

"Oh, good. You're awake."

The voice came out of the dark, I could not tell from which direction. Who was it? I did not recognize the voice. I turned my head and peered into the black night.

"Where am I? What happened?" I asked. My voice came out in a croak. There was no immediate answer. I cleared my throat and tried again. "Did I stumble in the dark? I seem to have bumped my head." As I spoke I realized that the back of my head pounded with a steady throb. I tried to raise my hand to see if there was a lump but I could not raise my hand nor my arm.

"You dropped like a log." The voice came out of the dark; it seemed amused. "I really didn't hit you that hard. You just went down like a log."

A chill froze my innards. "Is that you, Kegleigh?" Was I kidnapped by Harry Kegleigh again? Who else would treat me with such cavalier disrespect? Had I been so distracted as to let my guard down? I felt a wave of disgust with my lack of judgment.

I heard movement in the dark, but I could not see Kegleigh's broad form.

"Now why should you think I am Harry Kegleigh, I wonder?"

A dark shape materialized in my peripheral vision.

"Have you reason to believe the gentleman would attack you? Of course, I've heard that he likes his play rough...." The voice dropped.

The shape moved a little closer. I could not see who it was.

"Or could it be he took offense at that absurd masquerade of yours, pretending to be Arabella's ghost. May I ask, what was the purpose of such maudlin trickery?"

"Who are you? Show yourself, if you are not a coward." I let my disdain be known. "At least Kegleigh would not hide in the shadows," I added.

A post pressed into my back, holding me rigid. I realized that I was sitting upon the sand, tied to a post, my arms bound to my sides. A wharf, no doubt. We were beneath a wharf, where the night stars and the moon were excluded. No wonder I couldn't see a thing.

"I am sorry," the voice said. "I should have introduced myself. Ephrata Phinny, Esther's son. It will do no harm to tell you that."

The certainty with which he spoke made me shiver. He meant me harm; therefore he didn't care if I knew his name. I must keep calm and keep him talking. I needed time to figure out what to do.

"Froggy." I stated this name as a fact.

"Don't call me that." The man spoke in a cold voice. "Only *she* called me that, "he added, emphasizing the feminine pronoun.

I knew at once that he referred to Arabella Edwards . I was in the hands of her murderer. I took a moment to compose myself before I spoke.

"Why did she call you Froggie?" I asked, curious, even though I also meant the question to keep him talking.

"Oh, she had her little names for everyone. I was her pet frog... I leaped to do her bidding."

I could barely make out the black shape of an arm, thrust out like a bat's wing. Did I detect a note of bitterness in his tone? Could I exploit that feeling to my advantage? I needed to find out more about his relationship to the dead woman. Perhaps it would be wise to change the subject. Put him off guard

"Which wharf have you tied me to?" It might help to know my direction.

"You've figured that out, have you? I expected you to know. You're quite clever, in your way. Too clever by half."

I wished I could see him; this disembodied voice was unnerving. It's much easier to judge an opponent's move when you can see his face.

"But I don't know which wharf," I said. He must believe that I was not *too* clever. If he thought he was smarter than me he would be less upon his guard.

"A wharf where your cries for help will not be heard," he answered, satisfaction plain in his tone.

"The one near Gibbs Lane, then." I spoke aloud. T his wharf had been abandoned years ago. Unfortunately for me, at least one of its posts held strong.

"Too clever by half," Phinny repeated.

I thought it odd that he sounded pleased with himself. But

then murderers are often odd. The dark mass of his shape loomed to my left; he seated himself next to me.

"I wish I could see you," I complained. "I can't see a thing under here. Don't you have a tinder box?"

"I do, but I've no wish to be seen. Oh, I don't care if you see me, for what good that will do, but I prefer to err on the side of caution as far as others are concerned."

I hated the smug, oily tone he used. I couldn't afford to anger him at this point, however. I knew I must keep calm.

"You could light a bonfire out here and no one would see it," I said, much afraid this was the truth. All decent citizens were tucked away in their beds. There were no houses in the immediate vicinity, either. I was on my own with a murderer, as isolated in busy Boston as if I were in the middle of the vast wildernesses of Maine.

"True," he agreed, "but there's an unusual amount of traffic about town tonight, thanks to your masquerade-play. How do I know your friend Kegleigh might not stumble upon us in his drunken wanderings? I doubt not but that he and his companion are out roistering in some back alley tavern. No, I judge it better to be safe."

"Harry Kegleigh's no friend of mine." I kept my voice calm but my ears were tuned to detect any emotion coming from this cold-hearted villain. Since I could not see his face, I must depend upon my hearing. The thought sustained me that Harry Kegleigh would be no friend of Phinny's when he found out that Phinny killed Arabella Edwards. Let all the great oaf's violence be visited upon this man; I hoped I would be there to see it inflicted.

Once more I switched subjects, back to the figure at the center of this man's obsession.

"Tell me about Arabella Edwards. What did she do to you to make you hate her so?"

The black shape stirred beside me. "I didn't hate her. I loved her." The man's statement hung between us, his gloom thick as the night.

"You *loved* her?" I was incredulous; I could not believe

him.

"I asked her to marry me," he said,

"You asked her to marry you?" My incredulity was sincere. I felt surprised and yet not surprised. Love is often a violent emotion. Many have killed for love, as well as for hate. So now we were close to a reason.

Phinny rose to his feet, like a dark wave rising and looming over me, even as I felt the bay waters lick at my feet. He shifted from side to side.

"I wanted to marry her. With me by her side she could take her place in society. No one could look down upon her. I offered her my name, my devotion and my protection." Again the arm shot out in a bat's wing.

"What happened?" I asked, curious in spite of my situation. The woman had rejected his proposal? A good name to a woman like Bella Edwards was an offer of immense value. I watched the dark mass that was Phinny recede into the night. His voice rose over the slap-slap of the waters.

"She laughed at me. She teased me. I could not afford her, she said. I could have provided for her in ordinary comfort, but that was not enough for Arabella. She said she provided for herself very well indeed, and she had no mind to marry me or any but a man of great wealth. Great wealth!" The man groaned, his bitter cry piercing the black night. "Her good name meant nothing to her beside the lure of gold!"

M'sieur Germaine came immediately to mind. Phinny, with his offer of marriage, might be able to compete with Kegleigh and Boynton, two men who would offer the woman anything *but* marriage. He was no match against the wealth of Gabriel Germaine. Here was a real threat to Phinny. If Arabella married Germaine, she would be raised to a different level of society, one that would remove her from Phinny's sphere. It was highly unlikely that M'sieur Germaine would allow his wife to associate with her former paramours.

The words of my mystery poet came to mind. I spoke aloud without realizing it:

Greed for gold did maul her,
She lies now in the gloom.
Her golden glow is dimned now
And hidden in the tomb.

"Did you write that?" I called into the darkness. The stamp of boots upon the sand answered me.

Words floated towards me from a distance. "No, but it's true enough."

It was with relief that I discovered this phantom was not my poet. The man who wrote those lines could not have killed his muse. I couldn't let Phinny leave me here in this situation, if indeed he meant to leave. I called again. "What was she like, Arabella Edwards? Come back and sit down next to me. I want to know all about her." That should bring him back. Few lovers can resist the urge to speak of their loves, as few murderers can resist bragging of their crimes.

The waves seemed to be getting louder. I strained my ears and finally caught a crunching sound. The black shape emerged from the night.

"What do you care?" The voice was weary.

"I do care. I've been trying to understand her, to understand why someone would want to harm her." I could have bitten my tongue as I spoke the words. It hadn't been my intention to remind him of what he'd done. That would only remind him of what he proposed to do to me.

"Everyone seems to have liked the woman," I added quickly. "They say she was witty and good company and beautiful...." I let my voice drop, encouraging him to continue the tale.

The black shape plumped down upon the sand near me.

"Beautiful! Oh, God...she was beautiful as Eve...as seductive as Lilith." The man's voice was thick with emotion.

My eyes having adjusted somewhat to the dark, I could make out the pale oval of his face. Two eyes burned like black coal in the night. He picked up a handful of sand, sifting it through his fingers. My hearing had become acute, straining as I was to hear what I could not see. Each grain of sand grated upon my nerves as they dropped. It sounded like the slither of a snake, and I do not care for snakes. The lap-lap-lap of the water as it licked at my heels also added to my sense of unease. The tide would come in faster and faster.

Chapter Twenty-six

"I didn't kill her, you know." Phinny said these words as if he were confiding to me as a trusted friend.

I could not control a sudden expulsion of air; a snort of derision, I confess.

"No, I didn't kill her. I just didn't save her." The voice was eerie in its calm assertion.

"Well, if you didn't kill her, if it was an accident, you must tell that to the magistrates," I said, praying to the Lord the man would listen to reason.

"The magistrates?" It was Phinny's turn to snort. "As if they'd believe what happened."

"What did happen?" I asked, to keep him talking.

"It was her idea, after all." Phinny shook his head. "I tried to dissuade her, but she would not change her mind." He threw a handful of sand upon the beach. "Bella was stubborn. She had to try everything she read in those disgusting, vile books of hers. Did you know she drew filthy pictures for Boynton's books?"

Phinny leaned towards me, his eyes like burning coal in his pale blob of a face. I pretended ignorance, muttering in the negative. Was it Phinny searching Arabella's house, looking for Boynton's lost illustration. Had he found it? I'd try to discover its whereabouts.

Phinny nodded with vigor. "She sketched vile and disgusting pictures to match the books. She said it was her duty to read the books so she could draw her art. She called it art. And she must try out whatever perverted practice she read about...." Phinny paused. "That had its excitement, to be sure," he continued. "I confess to relishing those lustful practices with her. She would tie my hands..."

"Spare me the details," I interrupted in haste. "When I asked you what happened, I meant at the gallows in Salem. How did the... err, *accident* happen?"

"Well, that was it, you see. She must go to Salem to see the witch hanged because she read in one of her books that hanging produces a particularly powerful sensation of...pleasure. Only there was such a crowd that we were not able to witness the effect as the witch swung. Bella was extremely disappointed."

I shivered at his sudden bark of laughter and was glad the dark hid my reaction. What a precious pair the two must have been! I confess that I enjoy a good romp, but to take your pleasure in the shadow of the hangman? Revulsion filled my veins. I forced myself to recall that the woman had been punished for her sins and was even now being judged by a Greater Power. My duty was to procure earthly justice for her. How I was to obtain this while tied to a post beneath a rotting wharf with the waves licking at my heels I did not yet know.

"Go on," I said.

"It was all her doing. We must go back to the gallows at night and I must bind her like the witch and place a hood over her head like the witch and let down the drop so she could experience this titillation for herself. I was to cut her down immediately. She would not listen to reason. I assure you I tried to dissuade her. I must do as she said or she would find someone else to do it for her. I had no doubt she would enlist another man's assistance, so I did as I was told. Except for the last part." He jumped up.

I heard a splash as he took a step backwards into the dark. I could no longer make out his face and could barely distinguish his form. His words came ghost-like out of the night.

"I froze. It was a strange sensation, I assure you. I did everything she asked. I bound her, placed the hood over her head and let down the drop. I swear to you that I went to pull out my knife to cut the rope, but my hand refused to move. I saw her jerking below me, I heard her squawking like a chicken, yet my hand refused to move! Here was this beautiful woman, willing to satisfy my every craving, who asked little from me while others gave her fine clothes and jewels, and I could not move to save her! Strange."

He spoke in a voice of wonder, his words floating around me like the dark waters at my feet. The man was mad. I pulled in my slippers as close as I could to my body. I could not say a word.

"Oh, I've asked myself whether it was her refusal of my marriage proposal that made me stand there while she suffered, or her mocking of me, or her ordering me about like she did, but in truth none of those things seemed to matter at the time. I just stood there while she jerked about like a poppet on a string. That's what I remember thinking, how like a poppet she looked, jerking up and down and around and around. I didn't kill her, you see. I just didn't save her."

His words receded in the night; I heard sloshing steps as he walked away from me. Good, I thought, I'd rather drown in the dark than have him near me.

He called out a final time: "I'll be back when the tide goes out—I'll cut you loose then. They'll find your body and think you drowned." His mad laughter faded into the night.

I waited until I thought he was truly gone before I tried to release my hands. Wriggle my wrists as I might, the rope did not loosen. I tried to slide my hands upwards so that I could stand upon my feet and perhaps keep my head above water, but the rope would not budge. The waves were licking at my heels. Praying that the madman was beyond hearing me, I began to cry out.

"Ho! Help! Anyone! Help!" The chances of anyone hearing me were slim, yet might there be a fisherman out early or a laborer on his way to work? I called out at intervals, saving my voice for longer and louder shouts. In between calls, I examined my sins and asked the Lord to pardon each and every one. Since I had much to confess, I expected this course would take hours that I did not have, since the waves now drenched my thighs. Much to my astonishment, the Lord in His great mercy spared me the full recital. Out of the darkness above there appeared an angelic face, halo-framed and glowing in joy.

"Sweet messenger," I gasped, nearly swooning with rapture at the thought of a lowly sinner like me, Redeemed and called to Rapture by the very angels of Heaven. Me, Hetty Henry, carried into the presence of the All Mighty by His cherubs? Me, Hetty Henry, sitting in the company of those worthy Boston Saints John Cotton and Richard Mather? I closed my eyes, preparing my soul to be Received among the Elect.

"Lead me to the Father," I prayed.

And the angel voice sang out: "He is here! He is here!"

With great exultation I awaited my Redeemer. I heard a loud splash—did angels fall upon the water like wild geese? I felt my bonds slipping from me and I was free! My body was swept up and lifted unto the Heavens—and plunked down upon the rotting wood of an old wooden wharf. What, was I found wanting so soon? I had yet to face the All Mighty Judge! My eyes flew open.

"Hetty, are you all right?" The elfin face peered into mine while a small hand grasped my shoulder.

A bulky shape hauled itself up and over the wharf's edge beside me. Was I consigned to the nether regions, then? Was this Satan's creature come out of the deep to claim me from the very arms of Heaven? I was a sinner, none knew better than me... and at least it would be warm down there in the Fires. I found myself shivering from the cold as my sodden clothes clung to me in clammy folds.

The small hand shook me; it's tiny claws dug into my shoulder. Here was indeed an imp of Satan. "Ouch," I snapped. "Stop it, Celia."

"Oh, good." Celia set down the lantern she held in my face. "She is all right." Celia addressed the hulking figure beside me. "Hetty, this is my father, John Edwards. I'm sorry I didn't get here sooner but I had to run all the way to his house and wake him up and he must dress himself and follow me and it was hard to find my way back.... Where is 'Phalet? He was supposed to stay here with you. It's a good thing you shouted, Hetty. That helped us find you. Now where has 'Phalet gone off to...? Oh, wait, I think I hear something. It's him, I hear his whistle. He says it's a bird but I never heard a bird like that in London."

My head spun at her chatter. I was cold and wet and tired; I couldn't understand her nonsense. But I did hear the clatter of horse hooves on wooden planks and I recognized the Ferret's sharp hail. The huge shape beside me jumped up. Voices of men penetrated my fogged brain while Ferret danced up and down before me. I was not yet convinced this was not Satan's Domain.

"I brought Mister Kegleigh when Celia didn't come back, 'cause he lives close by. He's going to beat that bad man into a pulp and I may watch!"

I was dimly aware of being lifted bodily from the planks. Hands threw a large, warm cloak over my wet one and I was handed up to strong arms and a broad chest.

"I'll hunt him down and kill him." Pleasant fumes of rum surrounded the words.

My understanding was rapidly diminishing in drowsiness as I settled back in my safe haven, yet I found the strength to murmur: "You don't have to hunt for him, he's coming back when the tide goes out. He's going to cut me loose and let everyone think I drowned." There, the words were out. I yawned.

"The murdering bastard!" Fumes of rum puffed around me. "I'll beat him 'til he wishes he were dead."

"That's good," I said, feeling warm and comfortable. "Beat him and turn him over the sheriff in Salem. That man likes to hang people." I closed my eyes, lulled by the rocking motion of the horse.

I woke to a room full of people, all staring at me.

A voice to my right spoke. "You see? I told you she only needed to sleep." Doctor Geoffrey Malbone beamed down at me. "You're as strong as an ox. Nothing wrong with you at all. How do you feel?"

"Hungry," I said. I pulled myself up into a sitting position. Wherever I was, it was a fine bed with white sheets and white pillows and a fine white coverlet. Celia sat at the bottom of the bed. She patted the coverlet.

"I slept here beside you, Hetty. Harry said I was to be your nurse and take care of you."

"Harry?" Who was Harry? I turned my eyes to a fair-haired man with thick shoulders and a pleasant face. He was dressed in a linen shirt and a striped waistcoat. The man's blue eyes were on Celia.

"That's not Harry—that's my father. Don't you remember? He cut you loose from the wharf." Celia reached out and claimed the man's large paw within her own small fingers.

I looked at the man more closely. He ignored me, his attention on the small figure below him. His face glowed with pride.

"You...you're the poet, aren't you?" As I pointed at him the sleeves of my nightdress covered my hand. "You wrote that poem about Arabella."

I wanted to find out more about the man but my attention was claimed by a thin-faced youngster in a clean white shirt and brown cloth coat with horn buttons. I frowned, thinking the young man looked familiar.

Celia broke into merry peals of laughter. "That's 'Phalet, Hetty. Mrs. Wilfred made him wash up and comb his hair. She gave him a suit that her grandson's outgrown. "

"Fer... Eliphalet?" I was struck at the transformation of

my former spy.

The thin face broke into a wide grin. "Harry hired me to help Mrs. Wilfred. I'm going to live here. Shall I tell Mrs. Wilfred to bring you something to eat? She said as I should call her when you wake up."

"Please," I said and watched in bewilderment as the boy strode from the room. Where was I? Some form of Heaven, after all? A lower room, like Pergatory only with steps leading Upwards? The Ferret with scrubbed face? And this Mrs. Wilfred the Keeper, like Saint Peter? I shook my head to clear the cobwebs.

Celia giggled at my obvious amazement. "He likes Mrs. Wilfred. She feeds him cakes all the time."

"Who is Mrs. Wilfred?" How long had I been asleep, anyhow? What strange world had I entered? I looked up at Doctor Malbone. Here was a sensible man, at least.

"She's Kegleigh's housekeeper. You've been his guest...they've all been his guests since he brought you here. Harry's away in Salem. You remember what happened." Malbone's calm tone reassured me.

"Of course I remember. I'm glad he took Phinny to Salem, then. Let there be a legal end to this business." And let the bugger be hung for it, I thought to myself. I leaned against the pillows.

"We heard every word he said to you, that bad man. We were hiding up above on the wharf, Hetty." Celia bounced up and down on the bed in her enthusiasm. She still hung on to her father's hand. We told the magistrate all about it, 'Phalet and I. We had to sign a paper. It's a good thing I taught 'Phalet how to sign his name. He didn't want to learn but I made him. Now he's glad."

"How long have I been sleeping?" So much seemed to have gone on, and I slept through it all. Still, I felt wonderfully rested and ready to eat the ox I was as strong as.

The doctor answered. "Harry brought you here two nights ago. Well, what was left of the first night, anyhow. He sent for me immediately but I could see that you only need to sleep.

You'd suffered no harm from your dunking whatsoever."

The good doctor's reassurance pacified me. I turned to the gentleman on my left, whom I'd noticed but saved for last. He had stood by my bedside with great patience. I held out my hand.

"Creasy!" He took my hand in his long fingers. There was no need to speak of the happiness I felt upon seeing him. His scarecrow face was a welcome sight indeed. I could see the lines of worry disappear from his forehead as I greeted him. He would worry like an old woman about me, there was no help for it. And this time I'd really given him something to worry about!

The doctor interrupted before I could say anything further. "I think the lady has had quite enough company for the moment. Let us give this gentleman a chance to converse with her, if you please." He gestured to the door, moving back as he spoke.

Celia began to protest but her father, the Poet, held out his arm and she jumped off the bed to accept it. (Her father? I must find out about that!) The looks the man and child exchanged were full of pride and happiness.

Malbone winked as he closed the door.

"You're really well, Hetty?" Creasy leaned towards me, his dark eyes examining my face.

"Perfectly well, Creasy. I'm the same as when you left." I hastened to reassure him. Sometimes he was worse than a mother hen. "What happened in Salem? How did it go with you?" Best to divert him with questions.

"I bring good news, at least. The charges against you have been rescinded by the Salem magistrates. You're a free woman, Hetty."

"Oh!" I squeezed his fingers. "Creasy, I can't thank you enough for this service!" I felt as if an anvil had dropped from my shoulders. I was free to resume my own life! No skulking around in disguise, no more worry about cheating the hangman...I'd been prepared to flee the colony rather than risk hanging for a witch. It came to me how much I valued my life in Boston and my farm in Rumney Marsh. Friends, companions in work, the comfort of my religious advisors, my dear Cousin Abigail... even Cousin Cotton Mather, her husband; I would be loathe to part with such treasures. And these were the true treasures. My business interest I could transfer to another colony, but I could not part with these.

My companion cleared his throat. "I wish I could take the credit, but I can't. I did persuade Sarah Stiles to recant her testimony but that wasn't enough for certain of the justices in Salem. What really persuaded them was the letter from your lawyer threatening to sue them all for libel." Creasy shook his head. Stubborn old justices. "By the way, Sarah Stiles was paid by her cousin to turn you in with that ridiculous tale of hers. Guess who is her cousin?"

He answered his own question before I could speak.

"Ephrata Phinny, that's who. He asked her about you and she told him about her winter visit. I expect he embellished the story in her mind until she saw wolves and Satan and who knows what."

I laughed. "It doesn't matter now. Just remind me to give my lawyer a reward for that letter. "I squeezed his hand again. "So you discovered the wretch before we did! I take it you've uncovered the whole story, including what went on here."

Creasy nodded. "The children were quite proud of your little scheme to frighten everyone out of their wits. " This time he shook his head in disapproval. "Hetty, you are so rash sometimes! If you'd only waited for me...."

I hung my head and started to apologize to pacify his feelings but he went on, ignoring me.

"I had no real proof that he'd murdered Arabella Edwards, though I surmised the identity of 'Froggy.' I talked to the young kitchen maid, Susan, but she could add nothing more to what she'd told you. I went to the sheriff's office with my suspicions, however, and discovered Harry Kegleigh there before me. Phinny confessed to the sheriff. Harry told me what he'd done to you and where I could find you. I took the fastest boat back to Boston." He pressed my hand.

Since Creasy was no seaman—he hated sailing—I appreciated his concern.

"You'll have to give a deposition against Phinny but you can do that from here," Creasy continued. "You don't have to travel to Salem."

I had not the least desire to travel to Salem but I didn't want to appear a coward. "If they need me, I'm prepared to testify in person," I said. "In fact, as soon as they bring me something to eat I'll get dressed and go home. I didn't know this was Kegleigh's house. I fell asleep before we got here." I grabbed a second pillow and shoved it behind my back.

Creasy mumbled something inconsequential. I got the impression he had no objection to my leaving Kegleigh's house.

A knock on the door announced Celia's arrival. She bore with care and confidence a shiny tray which she set upon a small table beside the bed. The tray contained a steaming bowl of chowder and Johnnycakes golden with melted butter. There was a small blue pitcher of cider and a cup, too.

"I am your nurse and you must eat this food," she announced. "It's good for you." She turned to Creasy. "Sir, you are welcome to join the others. They are eating in the kitchen. There's ham and beef and such."

Creasy bowed his head to the child to acknowledge her civility but he told her he would keep me company for a little longer.

"I want to stay myself," Celia announced. She perched herself upon the edge of the bed like a little goldfinch. "I must make sure Hetty eats or I shan't be a good nurse. Mrs. Wilford says a good nurse always makes sure their patient takes some nourishment."

I lifted the tray and hoisted it upon my lap. Droplets of cider slapped over on the bright tray. "I have to obey my nurse," I said, grabbing a spoon and making short work of the chowder, the johnnycake and a mug of cool cider.

"My, I am a good nurse," Celia marveled. "I slept right

here beside you, Hetty. Harry said I must watch over you. Only I did get up yesterday while you slept. Children don't need as much sleep as old people. I helped 'Phalet settle in. He has his own little bed behind the chimney where he'll keep warm at night and his own little chest for his clothes and his treasures. Mrs. Wilford gave him her grandson's clothes to put in the chest. He has a wash basin and pitcher and soap, too. Mrs. Wilfred is strict about keeping clean. 'Phalet don't—doesn't mind, though. He'll do anything she wants so long as she gives him cakes to eat."

The child caught up her knees with two hands and rocked as she chatted on. "I think 'Phalet likes living here. I won't see as much of him, and I'll miss him, but when Aunt Meg arrives with the children I won't have so much time to play anyway."

"That reminds me, young lady." I broke in without remorse. "What about your father? Why didn't you tell me he was here in Boston?" Here I'd fretted about her being an orphan and that my duty would be to take her into my care, and she had a perfectly good father to look after her. Why had she hidden this little tidbit from me? I felt disgruntled, but on the other hand, she was a resourceful little thing. If she and Eliphalet hadn't followed me to the old wharf, I might still be out there floating in the bay.

"Oh, only Mr. Boynton was to know about my father. The grown-ups kept quiet for some reason." Celia tossed golden curls. "My father is a fine engraver, you know. Mother wanted to work with him on her pictures but she didn't want to be a wife to him any more. She and Mr. Boynton sent for him. Then my mother died and he was very sad. He wanted to find out who killed her. Papa thought it would be best if the bad man didn't know about him, so I promised to keep it secret. He didn't know I was coming to Boston, but he was so happy to see me!" Celia beamed, her small face looking very angelic.

I recalled the halo of her face bent over the wharf—no wonder I'd thought her a Heavenly messenger! Of course it was the lantern light, but she was as welcome a sight as any angel.

"Your father's an engraver...." My voice faltered as a thought struck me. "You know your mother drew pretty pictures for Mr. Boynton, Celia." I sincerely hope the child hadn't seen these pictures!

Celia's golden curls bobbed up and down in reply. "Of naked ladies," she said. "Mr. Boynton liked those best."

So much for my hopes, I thought. I leaned towards her. "You're an intelligent child, Celia. You found your mother's diary for me. Did you find the new picture that your mother made? Did you give it to your father, perhaps? I think it's what that bad Mr. Phinny wanted."

Celia shook her head. "No."

"Oh," I sighed in disappointment and sank back against the pillows.

"I gave it to 'Phalet. He liked the lady in it."

I sat bolt upright. "Does 'Phalet have it here?"

"It's one of his treasures. He has it in his box." Celia raised pale golden brows and cocked her head as if to inquire what I meant by my questions.

"Would you please go get 'Phalet and ask him if he will show us the picture? I think it's important."

Celia hopped off the bed and scampered out the door before I could turn to Creasy.

That gentleman hissed: "Is this the type of picture a young girl and a boy should see? Had we not better take it away from them? At least we must ask the father to hide it from their eyes."

While I sympathized with his shock, I thought it was a little too late hide things now. "Let me handle the boy, Creasy, if you please. I think this may be the reason Phinny killed Arabella Edwards."

Creasy sputtered a few objections but I knew he was as curious to see Arabella's latest work of art as was I.

Both children entered the room. A clean and combed Eliphalet advanced, holding a rolled sheet in his hand. I caught a glimpse of pink ribbon as he extended the roll to me.

"Thank you," I said, accepting the paper. My late spy shifted his feet; he kept his eyes on the floor. I untied the ribbon and unrolled the paper for Creasy to see. He gave a hasty glance at the children. In my opinion, the picture was not as lascivious as others I'd seen, and it was certainly well drawn. Still, for Creasy's sake I shielded it from the children.

A young man and a young woman were portrayed waist-high in a tranquil pond. Flowers arched over the banks, mirroring the arch of the woman's back as her nether limbs were wrapped around the young man's waist. Her long, dark hair trailed in the water while her lovely face with its thick black lashes glowed with sublime delight. Her delicate gauze garments clung to her bosoms, which sight drew the admiring gaze of the man, whose strong arms held her safe in her arched position.

A broad lily pad held a giant frog, its bulging eyes leering at the young woman in a particularly lustful manner. There was no mistaking the facial features of the amphibian; it was Ephrata Phinny. I turned to Eliphalet.

"Mr. Boynton's been looking for this. He'll pay you well for it. May I give it to him?"

'Phalet lifted his eyes from the floor; his brow cleared. I thought he seemed relieved. He nodded his vigorous consent.

"Is that all right with you, Celia?" After all, it was her mother's drawing. "Mr. Boynton did commission the picture from your mother—that means he asked her to make it for him."

"I don't care." Celia shrugged her thin shoulders. "It's 'Phalet's and he can do what he wants with it."

"Good," I said. "Now I hear that Mrs. Wilfred makes excellent cakes. Would you both be so kind as to bring some for Mr. Cotton and myself? I'm still a trifle hungry, you see."

'Phalet whispered something in Celia's ear and the children ran off.

"This picture puts Phinny in Salem at the time of Arabella's murder." I looked up at Creasy. "This is Froggy. No wonder he searched for it."

Creasy took the picture from my hand and examined it. "Not very flattering to him."

I agreed. "Perhaps it was the last straw. She laughed at him, ordered him around, refused his offer of marriage and mocked him with this picture for everyone to see. He told me he didn't kill her, he just didn't save her." I related Phinny's conversation as best I could remember. The dark and cold of the wharf seemed far distant from this cozy bed.

Creasy shook his head. "I can't leave you alone for a minute without you leapfrogging into hot water."

"Actually, the water was cold and I nearly croaked," I said. Word-play always put him in a good mood. Better than listening to him scold.

"Perhaps you had a frog in your throat." Creasy kept a straight face.

"I was hopping mad," I countered.

"I toad you to stay out of trouble."

"Well, it was dark and froggy out—I couldn't see or he wouldn't have caught me."

"Warts the use of complaining; the slimy thing will come to a fishy end."

I stifled a giggle. "More of a finny end, I'd say."

The door swung open with a bang. Celia and Eliphalet entered with plates of cakes.

"Here come the tadpoles," Creasy said.

I broke into gales of laughter; he chuckled.

"Grown-ups." Celia's golden brows drew together in a frown of disapproval. "They're silly."

M. E. Kemp lived an uneventful, happy life in Oxford, MA., the town her ancestors settled in 1713. Her grandmother's tales of family history from the Civil War to the Gold Rush and her father's penchant for trips to historic sites made American history every bit as colorful and bloody as European history to Kemp. She also enjoyed reading the medieval mysteries of Brother Cadfael and decided to create two nosy Puritans from Boston as American counterparts. This was after years of writing textbooks and magazine articles and teaching nonfiction writing in local colleges.

Her first book in the series introduced Hetty Henry and Creasy Cotton to readers. Hetty is a wealthy widow with connections to high and low society; Increase "Creasy" Cotton, a young Boston minister, knows how to ferret the guilty secrets out of the human soul. Her book, *DEATH OF A DUTCH UNCLE*, published by Hilliard and Harris, found the two Puritans in Dutch Albany with a rollicking cast of odd characters. *DEATH OF A BAWDY BELLE* is set during the hysteria of the Salem witch trials. In real life Kemp runs a dance program for mature adults and hopes to incorporate Colonial dance in her next mystery. Meanwhile she writes short stories, some of them with Hetty and Creasy and some of them about the 'Wobblies'—the IWW labor movement of the early 1900's. A firm believer that human nature doesn't change, Kemp notes that the same things being said against today's immigrants are the same things that were said about the immigrant ancestors of the bad-mouthers.

Over the years Kemp's many sojourns in old bookstores across New England resulted in a library of historical resources that she uses for her historical mysteries. She finds inspiration in the tattered and worn histories of the past and in the works of the much-neglected social historian, Alice Morse Earle. Kemp is a member of Sisters in Crime, New England chapter and Upper Hudson chapter; the Adirondack Center for Writing; the Hudson Valley Writers Guild and the Popular Culture Association. She lives in Upstate New York with husband Jack, (who hand-sells her books at OTB—some of her best customers are bookies!) and their two cats, Boris and Natasha.

www.mekempmysteries.com